Humans are so slow! Did I have to spell it out for her?

I decided I did. But just as I started to twist my tail into the shape of a P, she nudged me toward the door. My disappointment about the food was quickly forgotten when I realized she had set the shiny shoes down near the door. Now I could finally find out what they smelled like!

Scampering over, I stuck my nose down inside the nearest one and took a deep whiff. Everything got blurry for a moment as I inhaled the scent of frog water, snakeskin and dried roots I could not even begin to name. What could possibly smell like all of the those things at the same time? It was a powerful combination, and as soon as I felt normal again, I was ready for another sniff. The second time, the aroma was even more intense.

As I leaned in for a third sniff, Dorothy snatched the shoes away. I stared at her in disbelief as she kicked off her torn-up loafers. Was she going to put on the creepy frogwater shoes?

She was. Before I could utter a single bark of protest, she slid the shiny shoes onto her feet. Oh, no! Now Dorothy would turn into a dark, shriveled smelly thing like the one we'd crushed with our house. Desperate to show her her mistake, I rolled over onto my back and stuck my paws up in the air to demonstrate what could happen to her if she kept the shoes.

She thought I just wanted a tummy rub.

TOTO'S TALE

as told to

K.D. HAYS
&
MEG WEIDMAN

ZUMAYA THRESHOLDS   AUSTIN TX

2010

TOTO'S TALE

© 2010 by K. D. Hays and Meg Weidman

ISBN 978-1-936144-61-7

Cover design and illustrations © April Martinez

"Zumaya Thresholds" and the dodo colophon are trademarks of Zumaya Publications LLC, Austin TX.
Look for us online at
http://www.zumayapublications.com

Library of Congress Cataloging-in-Publication Data

Hays, K. D.
  Toto's tale / K.D. Hays and Meg Weidman.
     p. cm.
  Summary: Dorothy Gale's little dog, Toto, relates their adventures in the land of Oz from his point of view.
  ISBN 978-1-936144-61-7 (trade paper : alk. paper) — ISBN 978-1-936144-62-4 (electronic : alk. paper)
  [1. Dogs—Fiction. 2. Characters in literature—Fiction. 3. Fantasy. 4. Youths' writings.] I. Weidman, Meg. II. Title.
  PZ7.H314922Tot 2010
  [Fic]—dc22

                                        2010020451

This book is dedicated to all those—canine and otherwise—who are looking for a home. There's no place like home.

And to Terry (1933-1945), who will forever be "Toto."

WE'D LIKE TO THANK:

Catherine Asaro for her encouragement, support and the great introduction; experts Karen Freiberg, Rebekah Kaufman and Ali Schilpp for their helpful feedback on the manuscript; our terrific editor Liz Burton; writing friends Kathy Affeldt, Christie Kelley, Kathy Love, and Janet Mullany; the supportive students, faculty and staff of Sudbrook Magnet Middle School; Terry, the cairn terrier who brought the character of Toto to life so vividly in the MGM film *The Wizard of Oz*; and our own dogs, Alice and Shannon who always take great care of their pet humans.

Most of all, we'd like to thank family and friends for the help and inspiration along the way. This book would not have been finished without you!

Introduction

I met Toto at a fantasy convention in El Dorado. He was chasing my cat across the hotel lobby, so I'm embarrassed to say that my first words to him were somewhat less than cordial.

But he apologized for knocking over my luggage, and I apologized for allowing my cat to corner him under a sofa, and after that, we became friends.

Toto told me he was tired of being a cute sidekick at Wizard of Oz parties. And it bothered him that people didn't know the whole truth about what happened in Oz.

I'm glad he finally got the chance to set the record straight.

--Catherine Asaro

"But what do *you* want?" he continued, speaking to Toto. Toto only wagged his tail; for, strange to say, he could not speak.
— L. Frank Baum
The Wonderful Wizard of Oz

Chapter 1

I'd smelled fear on the humans all morning, and the stink was really getting on my nerves. I mean, we all knew a windstorm was coming, and it was going to be rough; but the humans didn't have anything to worry about. They'd just go down into The Hole and wait till it was all over.

It was the chickens who should have been worried. Their house was so flimsy it was likely to take off and fly away in the next windstorm. But chickens are too stupid to think about these things, so they weren't worried yet. Meanwhile, Auntem gave off enough worry scent to cover every living thing in the entire state of Kansas, and as I said, the smell was pretty annoying.

So, yeah, I knew I wasn't supposed to chase the chickens, but I couldn't help myself. When those lame-brained layers started bragging about which one of them could fly fastest, I decided to let them prove it.

I took off after Eggy, baring my teeth like I was going to rip all the feathers out of her tail. It felt really good to run. It also felt good to get some revenge on the chickens. Ever since yesterday, when the nasty old neighbor tried to stab me with a pitchfork just for digging a little hole in her garden, everyone here had teased me for running home with my tail between my legs. They would have done the same thing—it was a big *sharp* pitchfork, and the neighbor is as mean as a wet cat.

The chickens, in particular, had acted like I was the only one who had ever shown fear in the history of forever. Now I decided I'd put a little fear in the chickens so *they* could demonstrate why their name means being a coward.

"*Squahhhhh!*" Eggy yelled as she ran across the farmyard with me right on her tail. "That giant rodent is going to eat me!" Her big fat feathered body bounced ridiculously from side to side as she dashed around on long spindly legs.

"I thought you could fly," I barked. "And you know I'm not a rodent." I chased her into a corner between the water trough and the barn.

"I can't fly in this wind, you fool," she squawked.

"Excuses, excuses." I got ready to pounce on her, but she turned fast and hopped out of the way. Then she ran straight for the henhouse.

"Oh, no, you don't," I muttered as I shot after her. She would have to pay for that rodent remark.

The other animals always make rude comments about my size, but I think they're just jealous because I get to sleep in the house with the people. I'm small, yeah, but I'm a lot bigger than a rat. And I have a much nicer tail.

"He's coming this—*squaaah!*—way," one of the other chickens shrieked.

They had been pecking in the yard, trying to eat up all the loose bits of corn before they were blown away by the storm coming across the plains. Now, instead of eating, they scrambled frantically to get away from me, squawking and flapping and looking about as ruffled as they could possibly get. I loved it. I ran in circles, snapping occasionally to keep them moving.

Then I saw one obnoxious old hen who had pecked at Dorothy's ankle last week. I really did want to bite her. So, I opened my mouth extra-wide and headed straight for her big fat chicken butt.

"*Toto!*"

I had to stop when I heard that voice. It was Dorothy, my pet girl.

"Stop something chickens, Toto," she said.

With her flat face and small mouth, she can't really talk properly, but I still love her. Auntem and Unclehenry, the other people, are always making her work when what she really wants to do is roam the fields with me, chasing grasshoppers and digging for shiny beetles. She needs me to protect her from work. If you do too much work, you end up dull and sad like Auntem, or pinched and mean like the mean neighbor with the pitchfork.

I want to protect my girl and keep her just the way she is. I love everything about my Dorothy, from the smell of her shoes to her sloppy habit of throwing things everywhere. She throws a stick or ball, and I have to go pick it up for her. Then, instead of putting it away, she just throws it someplace else, and I have to pick it up again. It makes no sense at all, and sometimes I get tired of cleaning up after her. Still, I love her, and I'll do anything she asks.

When I *know* what she's asking, that is. I have to pay attention really hard to understand human speech, and usually, I don't bother

Right now, though, even if she didn't use many real words, I could pretty much tell what she wanted me to do just from the tone of her voice and the way she looked at me, as if she wanted to tie me up like a shock of wheat and throw me into the barn loft. She was annoyed, and I could smell a little anger on her, too. But underneath it all, there seemed to be more fear than anything else.

Fear of the storm, probably.

With one last look at the fat old hen, I turned and trotted over to Dorothy. I wagged my tail and hoped she would pet me for a minute and that I could help her forget her fears about the increasing wind and the dark clouds growing like mountains in the sky. Maybe she would also forget I'd been trying to scare the chickens and that I'd chewed on one of her shoes this morning before breakfast. She would forget it all, and we'd just...

It didn't happen.

She looked at me for a bit, like maybe she was going to pet me, but when she bent down, it was just so she could tuck a loose flap of leather back into her shoe. That piece of leather is always coming loose and tripping her, so she really should let me chew it off for her, but whenever I try, someone always stops me.

"Dorothy!" Auntem barked as she stepped out of the back door of the house, "Something up something chickens."

She can't talk any better than Dorothy. They practice a lot—it seems like they're always barking about something—but their language is so different it's difficult to translate into real words.

Anyway, I guess Auntem had just told Dorothy to round up the hens, because that's what she did. She ran around waving her arms, herding them all into the henhouse. I could have helped, but somehow I didn't think she wanted me to run around after them again.

So, instead, I trotted over to the barn to watch Unclehenry bring the cows and the horses inside. He was having a hard time holding the door open because the wind blew it closed. He kept turning to look over his shoulder, as if there were a monster behind him.

But it was just dark clouds and grass bent low under the weight of the coming storm. The wind moaned almost like a voice as it gusted along the eaves of the barn.

That sound made me shiver, and I had to admit I couldn't wait until it was time to go into The Hole.

The Hole is, well, a *hole*—dug out under the house—and since the house is very small, The Hole is even smaller. It's not much bigger than the ones I dig out in the yard to bury my pork chop bones. But it's deep and smells of worms and roots, a rich aroma that reminds me of underwear. It's a damp, comforting place much more interesting than the hard dry ground above. So, I never mind the wind and storms, because I know they mean a visit to The Hole.

With a loud thud, Unclehenry slammed the barn door shut and started toward the house with a lantern and pail of water. Maybe it was time already! I hurried to get Dorothy so we could go down into The Hole together.

I couldn't find her. The henhouse was closed up tight and sounded and smelled full of hens. I could tell Dorothy wasn't in there. She couldn't have gone into the barn, or I would have seen her. So, she must be in the people house. I pushed through the hole in the screen door, ran inside and headed straight for the door in the kitchen floor, expecting to see she was on her way down into The Hole.

She wasn't.

Chapter 2

Auntem was crouched down inside The Hole, crying.

"Toto!" Unclehenry yelled when he saw me. He reached out to grab my collar, but I twisted away from him. I had to find Dorothy, and I couldn't do that if they pulled me into The Hole.

Faintly, over the roar and moan of the wind, I could hear my name. Dorothy was calling me. *She* was out looking for *me*!

I ran toward the sound of her voice—out the kitchen door, down the steps and into the yard. At first, I thought she was in the front yard, so I headed that way. But the wind roared and swirled, carrying her voice in every direction, along with clouds of dust and straw. It was getting harder to see with each passing second.

I turned every which way, trying to find her scent or hear her call again. Then, just when I was afraid I'd never find her, I felt her arm around me. She scooped me up and carried me up onto the front porch. The wind pushed us back each step of the way. It seemed to take all Dorothy's strength just to get to the door, and then, no matter how hard she tugged, it wouldn't open. Wind whipped my hair into my eyes, and the roar made my head ache.

The full fury of the storm was almost on us now, and instead of being safe inside the wonderful Hole, we were out on the porch being attacked by flying bits of straw. I barked and wriggled out of Dorothy's arms to run to her bedroom window, which was open almost enough for us to crawl through. Dorothy was smart enough to understand right away what I wanted her to do. She pushed the window sash all the way up, set me inside then crawled in after me.

For a moment, we just lay on the floor together panting. The wind still howled and moaned, but the walls protected us from the grass and straw that stung like bees. We weren't in The Hole, but we were safe.

Or so I thought.

As the roar of the wind grew even louder, the whole house started shaking like it was tired of being attached to the ground and wanted to get up and move. That made both of us start crawling toward the kitchen so we could get down inside The Hole. Wind shrieked all around us like a demon, and the house was pitching and swaying so much it was hard to move forward.

Just as we reached the kitchen, the house gave one huge lurch, and everything tipped sideways. The roar of the wind was almost drowned out by a horrible ripping sound, as if the ground were being torn into pieces. We tilted the other direction, and I slid into a cabinet full of crackers, soup cans and jars of pickled eggs. Food? The food cabinets were too high for me to reach. How could I be seeing crackers? It made no sense.

Smells swirled by so fast the odor of henhouse poop mingled with the scent of the neighbor's apple pie. I thought I was going crazy. How could I smell the neighbor's pie when her house was 5280 steps away?

When I looked out the window, I saw why. The pie was sort-of hovering outside our window. And that wasn't the weird part. The weird part was that *we* were sort-of hovering above the ground. So was the henhouse.

The hens were not amused. Their feathers stuck out at all angles, and half of them were upside down. An egg hit the windowsill, leaving a stringy, gooey mess that stretched in a long line as the house spun around. Some got stuck in my ear. After that, the roar of the wind became less noticeable because I was too busy trying to rub the egg mess off my head. Every few seconds, I had to stop to watch for more flying eggs.

I watched for other flying things, too. After all, most of the smells of the farmyard don't come from eggs.

Dorothy wasn't watching as closely as I was, and she got hit in the forehead with a grade-A extra-large. She cried out in pain, and I ran over to her to make sure she was alright. I rubbed against her knee—I'm not tall, and when she's standing, that the highest part I can reach. She picked me up and held me against her cheek and whispered nonsense words. Together, we watched the chickens, hay, feathers and pie blow past the window over and over, like we were in the center of some weird merry-go-round.

The house had risen up to the top of a swirling cloud, which should have been very scary. And it was...for a while. Dorothy clutched me tightly, and my hairs all stood up and got itchy.

But things went on like this for so long, eventually it started to seem almost normal. Dorothy relaxed her grip on me. I relaxed my hair. She yawned. I yawned. She set me down. I didn't pay much attention to the window after that because I spotted a pork chop on the floor.

Or was it the wall? The reason I wondered was that the pork chop was lying on a picture of a grumpy-looking family. I didn't remember seeing pictures on the floor, but people did put them on the wall. Or maybe they grew that way. Anyhow, it was a small pork chop, so I finished it in a few bites and looked for a place to bury the bone.

There was an opening in the floor where the cellar had been when the house sat on the ground instead of floating. If I put my bone in there, it might keep up with the rest of the house and bury itself when we landed.

But what if it didn't? I decided to bury the bone in Dorothy's bed.

I guess she thought I was scared. She followed me and climbed onto the bed and poked around under the covers until she found me. We snuggled together for another long time, listening to the wind howl and feeling the house pitch and turn with a rocking motion that grew steadier after a while. It was way past time for my early-mid-late-morning nap, so I closed my eyes. Dorothy snored, but I never fell asleep. I did rest my eyes a little, though.

Suddenly, the bed fell out of the sky with a loud *whump* that hurt my ears. The house fell, too, of course, since the bed was still in the house. The view out the windows was different from back on the farm. I could see trees, lots of beautiful, tall trees. We don't have many of those back home, so it's hard to find a good stick to chew or the right target for marking territory. But now they were everywhere. I had never seen so many trees in one place.

"Dorothy," I barked, "I've got a feeling we're not in Kansas anymore."

But of course, she couldn't understand me.

Chapter 3

I ran to the door and barked to tell her to follow me, but she hung back, and I could smell that she was scared. I wondered if she was afraid of so many trees. Or maybe it was all the new smells. The wind brought the scent of rainwater, cherries, ground roses, clover, pie spices, apples and strange birds, plus lots of other things I couldn't even name. What could all of these new smells be? Where did they come from?

I was just about to start out the door without waiting for Dorothy when I realized some of those smells might come from large creatures that eat dogs. Enormous creatures with teeth the size of cattle horns.

I decided to go back to get my pork chop bone. Dorothy thought I was trying to hide in the bed, but I was just whimpering because I had a furball stuck in my throat, not because I was scared. Why should I be scared? After all, if there *were* enormous long-toothed beasts out there, they would eat Dorothy first because there was no way I was going out before her. She *is* my pet, after all, and is supposed to look out for me.

But she thought we were going out together, apparently. After pausing to tuck the loose piece of leather back into her shoe, she picked me up and carried me to the door, where the smells were even more powerful.

Sunlight filtered through the trees on a lush landscape of flowers and plants. I could hear birds that sounded like chickens, only less annoying. And there was a burbling sound that reminded me of Auntem pumping water into a tub for a bath. I would have to stay away from that sound. Baths in Kansas were bad enough. I had no intention of getting one here in this strange place. Wherever it was.

The difference became really obvious when three people appeared. I decided to call them "people-who-can't-quite-reach-things" because they were shorter than Dorothy, even though they walked and frowned like grown-up people who worked too much. I hoped these shorter people might store their food lower than the people in Kansas did.

These shorter versions of people were also mostly bald, and covered up their lack of fur with silly-looking clothes. They smelled terrible, and they had blunt teeth that weren't a whole lot longer than mine. So, I told them exactly what I thought of them without worrying they would eat me or trample me into the ground.

Dorothy clamped her hand down over my nose and stopped me in mid-bark.

When the people-who-can't-quite-reach-things got close to our house, they bent forward and looked down as if they were searching for something on the ground. Unclehenry, Auntem and Dorothy do something like this every night before supper, and I have never figured out what they're looking for. I used to think it meant they'd dropped some food under the table, but every time I looked, I never found any.

When the short people straightened up again, one—a female—stepped forward as if she were the leader of the pack. This surprised me, because in addition to being a female, she also looked awfully young to be the leader. But she was taller than the others, so maybe that made her important.

Then, when I looked at her more closely, I realized it was just her clothes that made her look young. She wore a light-colored dress, with a big frilly skirt and puffy sleeves, that reminded me of a lampshade. There was glittery stuff all over her, too, as if she'd sneezed into a pile of metal shavings. In the bright sunlight, she sparkled like pond water. When the sun ducked behind a cloud, though, I could see that under all the makeup she was wearing her face was wrinkled like a prune.

She was *old*, but she walked with pride, like she was important and she knew it and she knew that everyone else knew it, too.

"Are you a good something?" she asked Dorothy. "Or are you a bad something?"

This surprised me. Usually people just tell you whether you're good or bad. They don't ask your opinion.

Dorothy seemed surprised, too. She shook her head and barked some words that made it sound like she didn't understand what the old lady with the lampshade dress was talking about.

"You killed the something something," the Lampshade Lady explained.

"No!" Dorothy exclaimed in horror.

The accusation made no sense. Dorothy can't run fast enough to catch anything, and her teeth aren't sharp enough to kill anything if she did. And I'd been with her all day, and she hadn't even been mean to any living creature, let alone tried to kill one.

Maybe the Lampshade Lady was really talking to me, but I swear all I do is *chase* the chickens. I've never killed one.

The Lampshade Lady only laughed.

"Your house killed the something something, and that's good because something."

I sniffed around for signs of blood or gore. Did the house fall on the chickens? I wouldn't consider them good. And anyway, it wasn't like we asked the house to fall on anything. It just sort of happened.

I saw no signs of crushed chickens, but when I ran around the side of the house, I finally understood what the Lampshade Lady was talking about. Sticking out from underneath were two bony legs that looked like they'd belonged to a person about Auntem's size. At first, I had this sick feeling we *had* dropped the house on Auntem. Then I realized it couldn't possibly be Auntem because (1) her legs are stout, like an ox's, and the dead creature had legs more like a chicken's and (2) Auntem would never wear such fancy, shiny shoes. In fact, no one in the state of Kansas had shoes like that. Or legs like that. Just where the heck were we, anyway?

The Lampshade Lady led Dorothy around the house, and Dorothy shrieked when she saw the legs.

"Oh, no!" She turned and clutched at the lady's puffy sleeves. "Help! Something help her!"

But the Lampshade Lady just laughed. That was kind of obnoxious, I thought. I mean, our house had killed this person, so it wasn't all *that* funny. And the lady's laugh was real annoying, too. All high-pitched and squeaky.

"She was a bad something," the lady explained. She pointed to the east and then to the north and went on about being good. Then, with her face set in a grim frown, she pointed to the west, where the sun was already starting to sink toward the horizon. I couldn't understand what she said—except the word *bad* once or twice more—but just the tone of her voice made me shiver. There was probably a mean neighbor with a huge-normous pitchfork who lived somewhere in that direction.

Dorothy and the Lampshade Lady jabbered on for a while about good and bad things in various directions, but I figured I didn't need to pay attention anymore. Our house had killed the bad whatever in the east. So, if we just stayed away from the bad whatever in the west, we'd be fine.

I decided to go over to sniff the legs with the shiny shoes, but as the sun came out from behind a cloud and cast its rays over the side of the house, the legs started to dry up and shrink. By the time I got there, nothing was left but the shiny shoes.

I barked to get Dorothy's attention. She couldn't feel bad about killing something that wasn't even there anymore, could she? What *had* those legs belonged to? The smell in the shoes would give me a good idea.

But just as I turned back to get a whiff, the Lampshade Lady jumped over in front of me. She moved with amazing speed, almost like magic. Before I had a chance to get my nose in place, she reached down, plucked the shoes up off the ground and handed them to Dorothy.

I groaned. What a waste! Dorothy couldn't tell anything about them from the smell. And she hardly ever took the time to chew shoes, either. The Lampshade Lady should have given them to me.

Dorothy tucked the shoes under her arm without even trying to sniff them. She nodded toward the house.

"I need to get home to Auntem and Unclehenry," she said with a frown of worry. "Can you tell me how to get to Kansas?"

The Lampshade Lady and the other short people just sort of looked at each other for a moment. Then they all started talking at once, and though I didn't hear the word *no*, they all seemed to be saying it in one way or another. There was a lot of head-shaking and sour looks and pointing in various directions and gloomy low-pitched voices.

Dorothy didn't seem to believe them at first, but the longer they talked, the more I smelled fear rising in her. Tears welled up in her eyes and spilled over onto her cheeks, and soon she was sobbing. The others kept talking; but now instead of pointing in various random directions, they all started pointing at a road made of bricks. As if that would solve anything. We didn't have a car.

I don't know how they could keep talking when what Dorothy needed was a hug. Even I knew that, and I'd never hugged anyone in my life. I nuzzled her ankle, but without arms, I'm not much good at hugging. Auntem does it really well. Dorothy needed Auntem to give her a hug.

She also needed a tissue. I realized that when she picked me up and gave me a hug. Her nose was running like crazy, and as much as I love my girl, I really don't like the feeling of wet snot in my hair.

Still, I tried to ignore the wetness as Dorothy held me close.

The Lampshade Lady raised her hand, and the others stopped jabbering like they knew she was going to say something important. I concentrated real hard so I could understand.

"You must swallow the Jell-O brick road," she said with finality.

Now, that was something I could do. I licked Dorothy's chin to cheer her up. Jell-O was a little weird but definitely eatable. It might take a while to eat a whole road, but I knew I could do it. If that was all it took…

Wait a minute.

I turned to look at the road. Those bricks weren't Jell-O. They were bricks of bricky stuff—hard, heavy and non-edible. How were we supposed to swallow them?

Maybe I misheard that part. She probably said to *follow* the road.

But how was that narrow track of bricks going to help us? We'd flown here through the air. We couldn't just walk back. And there weren't any brick roads in Kansas, so this was probably going to lead us someplace else weird. If she'd told us to follow a *dirt* road, I'd have felt a lot more comfortable.

"Can you come with us?" Dorothy asked the Lampshade Lady.

"No." Then she said something about shoes.

Coward! She was as bad as a chicken and just about as ugly. She knew this place, and we needed her help, and she wouldn't help us. I was starting to get mad, really mad. I wriggled down out of Dorothy's arms ready to bite the Lampshade Lady, but she disappeared before my very mouth.

Chapter 4

I mean, she *really* disappeared. One moment, she was standing next to the house pointing at the shiny shoes she wouldn't let me chew, and the next she had completely vanished. Even her strange smell disappeared into the wind. I aimed my teeth at her ankle and ended up with a mouthful of prickly grass.

Actually, the grass probably tasted a lot better than her ankle would have.

I was so surprised I didn't even think to try to bite one of the short people instead. But I was mad at them for making Dorothy so sad.

She stared at the brick road for a long time. It curved through fields and woods and stretched far into the distance, and it went on for so long that it made me tired to just to look at it.

That was all Dorothy or anyone else did for a great while. Then, finally, with a big sniff, Dorothy turned and walked back into the house, still clutching the shiny shoes in her arms. I followed her, waiting for her to set down the shoes so I could smell them. The creature that had worn them, the ugly thing we dropped the house on, had smelled bad, but in a really interesting way, like the corner of the barn where they shovel all the horse poop.

Dorothy packed a basket with some dry hard crackers that tasted almost as bad as dog food. And she found a box of dried-up dark things that looked like shriveled junebugs but without the crunchy coating. While she packed, I kept hopping up and down, barking "Pork chop, pork chop," but she misunderstood and picked up half a loaf of bread instead.

Humans are so slow! Did I have to spell it out for her? I decided I did. But just as I started to twist my tail into the shape of a P, she nudged me toward the door. My disappointment about the food was quickly forgotten when I realized she had set the shiny shoes down near the door. Now I could finally find out what they smelled like!

Scampering over, I stuck my nose down inside the nearest one and took a deep whiff. Everything got blurry for a moment as I inhaled the scent of frog water, snakeskin and dried roots I could not even begin to name. What could possibly smell like all of the those things at the same time? It was a powerful combination, and as soon as I felt normal again, I was ready for another sniff. The second time, the aroma was even more intense.

As I leaned in for a third sniff, Dorothy snatched the shoes away. I stared at her in disbelief as she kicked off her torn-up loafers. Was she going to put on the creepy frogwater shoes?

She was. Before I could utter a single bark of protest, she slid the shiny shoes onto her feet. Oh, no! Now Dorothy would turn into a dark, shriveled smelly thing like the one we'd crushed with our house. Desperate to show her her mistake, I rolled over onto my back and stuck my paws up in the air to demonstrate what could happen to her if she kept the shoes.

She thought I just wanted a tummy rub.

Fortunately, whatever magic was in those shoes did not seem to affect her because she still smelled like Dorothy.

After a minute, she shooed me outside, stepped out, locked the door and put the key in the pocket of her dress. Then she started for the brick road, and I followed.

The Lampshade Lady was gone, but the others were outside talking in low voices and watching us suspiciously, as if they expected us to steal the bricks out of the road rather than walk on them. I turned my backside toward them and farted in their general direction.

The road was only about fifty steps away. It was wide enough for two horses, if they were harnessed close together, and it was made of crumbly old brick that left dust on my paws. Dorothy's new shoes made a clicking sound on the bricks. Actually, one of her shoes made a clicking sound. The other was more of a clopping sound. Click, clop, click, clop—I thought I would go crazy from all the noise.

So, instead of staring at the shining shoes or the road ahead of me, I tried to distract myself by looking at the countryside. It was flat like Kansas but with beautiful trees all around. I hadn't had time to mark any since we'd arrived, so I was hoping Dorothy would take a break soon. She's a little taller than me—okay, a lot taller—and I could barely keep up. If I stopped to claim a tree, I might lose her.

After a while, we came out of the forest into a village of odd little round houses. The people-who-can't-quite-reach-things who lived there stopped working and stared at me as if they'd never seen a dog before. I started barking just to see if I could scare them.

They laughed.

I hurried back to Dorothy.

On the other side of the village were fields of corn just like in Kansas. Big black crows circled lazily through the air and landed in great cackling clusters, just like in Kansas. And up on a stick in the closest field was a figure stuffed with straw in the shape of a person, just like in Kansas. I think it was supposed to scare away the crows, but I never saw any reason why birds would be afraid of a pile of straw that didn't move.

Then I nearly jumped out of my fur. This stuffed pile of straw did move. It nodded, and winked at Dorothy. I'm not making this up. It even said something in that weird language people use.

The nod could have just been a trick of the wind, but the wink? And the talking? No, there was something really strange about that straw man. It was haunted, full of ghosts just waiting to snatch our souls and take us off to the land of endless bubble baths.

"Dorothy!" I barked. "We've got to get away from this thing!"

She stopped in her tracks. "Did you talk?"

"Yes!" I wagged my tail like mad. At last! She could understand me. After all these years of miscommunication. "We need to get away from—"

She waved for me to be quiet. "Toto, hush, I can't hear what he's saying."

What *he* was saying? What about what *I* was saying? Since he was a haunted pile of straw, whatever he was saying would be a lie designed to trap her so he could steal her soul. What I was saying was much more important.

"Run!" I barked.

Since the straw man was attached to a pole, I didn't think we'd have to work too hard to get out of its reach. But just in case, after we'd run about twenty steps or so, I turned around to make sure it hadn't followed.

It hadn't.

Neither had Dorothy.

While I was making a very sensible escape, she stood in front of the thing, talking to it as if it were Auntem's cousin who had come for a Sunday visit. And then, to my horror, she reached up behind the thing and unhooked it from the pole.

"No," I barked frantically as I ran back. "Don't let him loose!"

But it was too late. The haunted pile of straw was now free to chase us or trap us or whatever it planned to do. Though I have to admit, the straw guy didn't look too dangerous at first, because as soon as Dorothy let him off the hook, he crumpled to the ground in a heap and just lay there, all tangled and twitching.

I kind of felt sorry for him—for a moment.

Then Dorothy reached out to help him stand up.

"Come down the hello brick road with us," she said to him. "Something the lizard can give you legs."

We were following this road to get to a lizard with extra legs? I wasn't sure this was a good idea at all.

The tangled Strawman laughed. "I have legs," he said. "What I need is a train."

"I'm sure the lizard can give you a train," Dorothy assured him. "So, come with us."

She promised that without any hesitation. I wondered for a moment if the lizard somewhere down that brick road could give me a pork chop.

Wait, did she said the lizard could give the straw guy a train? Or had she said "plane?" Either way, if the lizard could give us some major transportation, maybe we really could get back to Kansas.

But no, that made no sense. Lizards might have extra legs, but they didn't have planes or trains or even pork chops. Obviously, those shiny shoes *were* having some effect on Dorothy.

And anyway, even if it had a plane, the trip to see the lizard wouldn't be worth it if it meant we had to bring this haunted pile of straw along with us. He could barely even walk—he wavered and wobbled all around as if he'd never used his legs before. And that made sense because stuffed guys made out of straw aren't supposed to walk and talk. I tell you, this was *not* normal.

But Dorothy didn't seem at all worried. She just led him out to the brick road as if she escorted talking bags of straw every day of the week.

I wasn't going to stand for it. I could rip this guy to shreds with my bare teeth, and I'd do it, too, rather than see Dorothy fall under the spell of his evil magic. With lightning speed, I ran forward, grabbed hold of his leg and pulled with all my might.

Instead of being grateful, Dorothy scolded me.

"Let go, Toto!" she said sharply. It was the mean voice she hardly ever used. The voice she'd used when I was chasing the chickens. I probably deserved it then— I knew I wasn't supposed to chase those old feather-brains around. Yeah, Dorothy was right to scold me then.

But not now. Not when I was trying to save her from evil she had yet to understand. I couldn't believe she was being so foolish. Did she trust that walking itch-bag more than me?

Hurt and disappointed, I slunk back into the shadow of the tall cornstalks.

Dorothy turned away and started jabbering to the strawman. He laughed as he stuffed straw back into his pant leg. Then the two of them started down the brick road without even glancing back to see if I followed.

I did, of course. Not too closely, because I didn't want the unsteady strawbag to step on me, but I watched his every move. When he turned on Dorothy, I would catch him. And then she would realize she should have trusted me rather than him.

He definitely had straw where his brains
were supposed to be

Chapter 5

I couldn't tell if the scarecrow was completely stuffed with straw because I hadn't had the chance to give him a thorough sniff. But he definitely had straw where his brains were supposed to be because he acted like he had less sense than the corn he had been guarding. When we came to a place in the road where the bricks were missing, I jumped over the hole and Dorothy walked around it. Not Itchman. He stepped right into it, tripped and fell. I could understand his being a bit clumsy, but he did this over and over, getting back up with a laugh each time.

Finally, it was time to stop and eat. Dorothy stepped over to a tree stump, sat and put her basket on her lap. I knew she couldn't pull anything really good out of it, since she'd hadn't put anything much good in to begin with, but even not-good food is better than no food at all.

She handed the strawman a piece of bread.

"I don't eat," he said.

Well, that made sense. His mouth was painted on. And if he did eat anything, it would probably be straw rather than bread.

Which left more for us.

"Oh, okay." Dorothy nodded toward me. "Something feed it to Toto, then."

I hurried over to him eagerly and opened my mouth, but the strawman tried to put the food in my left ear! Even if he didn't eat anything himself, he should know from watching the crows that a mouth has a purpose that's much more important than making noise.

I jumped up to grab the bread from his hand, thus demonstrating the proper use of a mouth. My lunch was gone in two gulps. Then, while Dorothy talked to the strawman about Kansas and Auntem and Unclehenry, I prowled around the clearing where they sat, sniffing for signs of danger.

Since we'd left the cornfields where the scary straw bag had joined us, the country had grown more wild. There were fewer farms, and I saw no people, not regular-sized or the ones-who-can't-quite-reach-things. Even the trees looked less inviting than the ones we'd seen earlier. They were gnarled and scraggly, and had branches like twisted arms waiting to snatch up unwary puppies who strayed too far from their mothers.

I used to wish we had more trees in Kansas, but now I would have traded just about anything to be back there, even if I never got to mark another tree again. I guess you don't realize how much you like your home until you go away. There's no place like it.

We walked all afternoon. The gnarled trees grew closer together, until they formed a dark, twisted canopy overhead. Dorothy began to stumble, and her steps were less certain, as if she couldn't see where she was going. I dashed out in front, barking to show I would guide her, since I can see better in the dark than she can. She leaned on the strawman instead.

Dorothy needed to rest.

I needed to rest.

I can sleep anywhere, but Dorothy needed a house, so I started to search for one. By the time I finally found a tiny cabin, I was almost asleep on my paws. I smelled the cabin long before any of us saw it, of course. Wood cut into planks is dried out, not fresh like the wood in trees. I could smell ashes, too, the remains of an old cooking fire. And something else...was that frog water?

Chapter 6

We led Dorothy into the tiny wooden building littered with old leaves and mildewed straw. Compared to this, our little house in Kansas was like the huge Cow Palace at the State Fair. But Dorothy seemed not to notice the size, or the dampness, the stink of rotten planking or the lack of people furniture. She curled up on a pile of leaves and went to sleep.

The strawman stood at the door, as if he were keeping watch. But he might have been waiting to signal his evil straw army to attack. So, while I pretended to sleep at Dorothy's side, I kept watch all night.

Well, most of the night.

As long as I could, anyway.

Strawman was still standing by the door when Dorothy shook me awake. I smelled no food in the house, and though there were a few cans on a shelf, none of them had pictures of food on them.

"We need to go look for water," Dorothy announced as she opened the door.

"Why?" Strawman asked.

"To drink."

33

I started to follow her out the door, but her next words stopped me cold.

"And to wash up."

Wash? We don't need water to wash. That's why we have tongues. But humans don't understand this and live under the misguided impression that it's necessary to immerse yourself in water on a regular basis to get clean. It's dangerous and totally unnecessary, like using a lawnmower to trim your hair. If she was interested in washing, then I was interesting in being somewhere else.

So, as soon as we got outside, I headed in the opposite direction from the one she'd taken. I hoped that, long ago, some past resident of the house might have buried a pork chop bone in the woods nearby. With my nose to the ground, I searched all around the house in an ever-widening circle.

I picked up no scent of meat, just rotting leaves. We were in an old forest of tall trees with branches spread out to make a leafy canopy high overhead. I caught a whiff of some nuts, or acorns, maybe. Something I could eat if I was hungry enough, and I was.

The scent grew stronger, and I ran faster and faster until suddenly I wasn't running at all anymore. I hit something hard and smooth and very untreelike. It smelled like metal and was about as much fun to run into as metal. When I looked up, I saw that it was rounded like a small silo, but there were two of them. What was really weird was that they were joined together at the top and had something like arms coming out high above me, sort of like branches.

I stepped back. This was some sort of strange human-shaped beast, like the creature with the shiny shoes, but this guy had more rust than shine. I should have been scared; but the beast was very slow, which probably explained why we were able to hit one with our house. It moved so slowly, in fact, that it didn't appear to be moving at all. I think even with my short legs, I could probably have outrun it.

I realized pretty quickly that I didn't need to outrun him because he was as still and smooth as ice on the water bucket in winter. A frozen metal man. I licked him and found that he *wasn't* cold, so he wasn't made of ice. He did taste a little like the water bucket, but that's because the water bucket is made of metal and it had a lot of rusty spots, too, just like this guy.

He was holding his arms way up over his head, and when I stepped back to get a better view of him, I saw he was holding something sharp over his head. For a moment, I was stunned. How had I not noticed the giant axe hanging over my head? This metal man could have chopped me up like a hotdog.

But he didn't. Because he was frozen in place. He couldn't move at all.

I started to feel sorry for him. He was all alone with no one to pet him or help him scratch behind his ears. He had no one to snuggle with on a cold winter night. Since he couldn't bend, he couldn't have snuggled anyway, even if he had someone. He must have been very lonely.

"Toto?" Dorothy called from somewhere behind me.

"Come here," I barked as I ran back and led her to the metal man. "You gotta see this. At first, I thought it was a silo, but it's really a guy made out of metal who can't move at—"

"Hush, Toto," she scolded gently. "I can't hear him talk."

What? I thought he was frozen in place.

But his mouth could move just a little—just enough to make some squeaky noises. And apparently, those squeaky noises were clear enough for Dorothy to understand them, because she said, "Oh, okay," and started to look around for something on the ground nearby.

It wasn't fair! He could talk, too? How was it that strange people made out of non-people material could speak a language Dorothy could understand while I, who knew her better than anyone, could not? Since I had been paying more attention, it was getting easier for me to understand what she said, but the other way round wasn't working. Maybe she just wasn't trying.

"He needs some something," Dorothy said to Strawman. "Can you see if there's any in that little house?"

He scampered off like a wobbly puppet and soon returned with a can of something that was not food. Together, he and Dorothy poured stuff from the can on various parts of the metal man's body, like his knees and his elbows. The metal man began to bend his legs, and when they had poured stuff on his shoulders, his arms lowered suddenly and the axe thundered down so close it nearly shaved the hair off my behind. Everyone seemed to have forgotten I was there.

Dorothy put the stuff from the can on Metal Man's jaw, and his squeaking turned to regular human babble even I could understand a little.

'Thank you," he said in a rusty voice.

"Something stuck something long time?" Strawman asked.

"Oh, yes." The metallic face somehow twisted into a smile. "Something glad you came by."

"So are we!" Dorothy said as she wiped some rust from Metal Man's arm.

He turned to her. "Thank you, again. But why are you out here in the something woods?"

"We've been swallowing the hello brick road to find the lizard to get some trains," Strawman explained. Then he laughed. "For me, that is. Dorothy has trains. She just wants to get home."

Dorothy did not have a single train that I knew of. Or planes, for that matter. Strawman must be after something else besides major modes of transportation. Was it drains? Cranes? I sure wished he could speak properly.

"I'm hoping the lizard can help me get back to Auntem and Unclehenry," Dorothy explained.

I really didn't want to hear any more after that. Why did she think a lizard could help her get home? Why didn't she say "I hope the dog can help me get back to Auntem and Unclehenry?" Dogs can do a lot more than lizards, and she wouldn't have to follow (or swallow) a brick road to get me to help, either. All she'd have to do is ask.

Which she didn't.

I stopped paying attention to their jabber. I still hadn't figured out what Strawman hoped to get from a lizard down the road. The only thing he seemed to need was straw, and he could get that at any farm. Well, he probably could have used a *brain*, but it wasn't like we were going to find that lying somewhere down that road, now, were we?

I lay down and had just about drifted off to sleep when a horrible low noise nearly made me jump out of my paws. Strawman laughed. After a moment, I heard the sound again and saw what caused it—Metal Man was pounding on his chest. The ringing metal echoed with a deep bass thrum that shook me down to my pads. It was worse than the time Dorothy's cousin ran the tractor into the side of the water tank. Metal Man was as empty on the inside as a Kansas water tank in August. No straw, no hair, no blood and guts—just air.

Nothing to bite. And I was starting to feel like I really wanted to bite something, I was so annoyed. I had saved this metal man. He'd been trapped before I discovered him and led people to him, but he hadn't even so much as patted me on the head. And Dorothy spent so much time talking to him and Strawman she seemed to have no use for me at all. All our time in Kansas, I was her best friend, and we went everywhere together. Now, we were still together, but she had new friends she liked more than me.

I wish we were back in Kansas.

Chapter 7

Trees, I have decided, are not such great things after all.

We had been walking through forests for a long time, and all we ever saw were trees. And more trees. I was starting to hate them. Dark, drooping leaves rustled ominously all around as we passed, as if they were whispering about us behind our backs. Each tree trunk stood in silent, menacing blackness like the opening to the cave of some monstrous beast.

I was thinking a lot about monstrous beasts as we walked, actually. After all, I needed to think about something besides how much I missed Auntem's pork chops. But thinking about monstrous beasts was probably not a good idea, because now I was starting to imagine I could hear them, too. The low hissing sound that came through the trees probably was from something very large, maybe with five legs instead of four, and scales like a snake and the head of a giant cat with teeth the size of steak knives. Then there was this high-pitched squawk that made my fur crawl. I think it came from a bird like a carrion crow but much bigger, with talons strong enough to snap me in two.

I made sure to keep pace with Dorothy's footsteps on the uneven bricks, so I'd be ready to protect her if something should threaten her.

After a while, the squawking sound died away, but a low rumbling growl echoed through the forest behind us.

"What was that?" Strawman asked.

I wished I could say it was just my stomach growling, but my stomach isn't big enough to make that much noise, no matter how hungry I was.

"Just walk faster," Dorothy suggested. "Come on, Toto."

I tried to speed up, but at the same time, I was constantly turning around to try to get a glimpse of what was back there. Though I couldn't see anything, I could smell cat.

But I didn't know any cats big enough to make that kind of a deep growl.

Of course, we're not in Kansas anymore.

So, I probably shouldn't have been surprised when a cat the size of a tractor leapt out from the trees, snarling and gnashing his fearsome teeth. Standing on his hind legs, he must have been twelve feet tall, with massive claws and a big heavy tail that swung back and forth over my head like a whip.

I was scared hairless. So were the others—I could feel Dorothy shaking with fright and smell the pungent aroma of fear all around. Strawman, who was unsteady on his feet in the best of times, was quaking so badly his straw-filled knees knocked together. He tried to stagger away but stumbled instead and fell to the ground, skidding against the dried leaves on the brick road.

The Big Cat lunged toward him, but Metal Man stepped in front to block his path, waving his woodcutter's axe in the cat's face. Startled, the cat crouched back down.

Encouraged by his success, Metal Man waved his axe in a wild arc all around. But he got so wild he tripped over Strawman and went sprawling onto the bricks. He dropped his axe, and the axe head fell off the handle with a dull thud. So, he was pretty much useless.

"Oh, n-no," Dorothy cried. Even her voice was shaking now. I couldn't smell fear on the Straw and Metal Men, but they were obviously as scared as she was.

The big cat again raised himself to his full height and crept toward us, growling. I wanted to disappear into the underbrush. As much as I hated to admit it, that overgrown feline could eat me for dinner and still be hungry.

But I had to protect my Dorothy, so I charged straight toward his left rear paw, barking my head off to scare him.

It worked, too. At least, I thought it did, at first. He jumped away with a muffled cry of fear. But then I noticed he was holding his nose, and I hadn't hit him anywhere near that high.

"Don't you dare bite Toto!" Dorothy yelled, holding up her basket as if it were an attack club. She must have hit him in the nose with it. I knew that heavy stale loaf of bread would turn out to be good for something.

The big cat started to whimper like a newborn mouse surrounded by, well, cats.

"I didn't bite him," he moaned.

"No, but you tried to," Dorothy retorted. "You should be something something trying to bite a little dog."

I didn't like the reminder of my size, but I was thrilled to realize Dorothy had faced up to the big cat just to save me. Not that I needed saving, of course. I *am* a dog, and he *was* a cat, and in the end I would have chased him away. But she didn't know that. She acted to save me, despite her fear. She must still love me, at least a little.

I jumped up and licked her hand.

She patted me on the head, and I felt happier than I had ever since we came to this weird land over the clouds.

"He really is a little dog," the big cat said unhappily. He grabbed his own long, droopy tail and began to wrap it around his paw. "Only a cowgirl would try to bite such a little dog."

Strawman untangled himself, rolled up onto his feet and stepped over to him. "You shouldn't be a cowgirl. You're so big."

And, from the looks of things, he wasn't a girl, either. No cow, no girl—he must have said something else. Cowbird? Cow turd?

"How could you be a cow turd with such big paws?" Metal Man wondered as he clinked and clanked into a standing position.

The big cat sniffed—and it was a wet, gurgley sound that meant he had a nose full of snot. Tears spilled out of his eyes. I hoped he wasn't going to wipe his nose with his tail because that would be really gross.

"I don't know why I'm a cowbird," he wailed. "I just am!"

Dorothy stopped being mad at him then. She and the other two started to try to comfort the blubbering beast. They all came up with different reasons why he was such a whatever he was.

I don't know what he was worried about. As far as I could tell, he had way more than one problem. He was a scaredy cat with a compulsive tail-wringing disorder, dandruff, stinky feet and probably a minor case of ADHD. All the time they were talking, he kept pointing out strange bugs and animal tracks in the dirt.

Of course, he could talk to the others, and that made them see him as one of them.

Unlike me, whom they tended to ignore.

"You should come on the hello brick road with us," Dorothy suggested. "The lizard could give you some porridge."

"Really?" the big cat asked hopefully. "Do you really think he could—oh, look at the tongue on that chipmunk. Do you think it bites?"

"You wouldn't be able to feel it if it did. Its teeth are too small," Strawman pointed out.

"But it does have big feet," Metal Man added.

We all both looked at him. The chipmunk's feet were about the size of an acorn top.

"For its size, I mean," Metal Man continued somewhat defensively. "If he stepped on another chipmunk's foot, it would really hurt."

"Why are we talking about chipmunk feet?" Big Cat asked.

Strawman pointed at him. "You brought it up."

Dorothy shifted from side to side uneasily as she tried to get their attention.

"Um, do you think we could—"

The Big Cat stretched up tall and crossed his paws in front of his chest.

"I never said a thing about its feet."

"Dorothy," I barked. "Let's forget these guys and just move. They could be here all night arguing."

"What I think he's trying to say," Metal Man said in soothing voice, "is that *you* first pointed out the chipmunk."

Dorothy waved with her arms outstretched, and still they didn't pay any attention to her. Finally, she gave up, turned on her heel and started down the brick road.

"Come on, Toto," she called over her shoulder.

I hurried after her joyfully. I don't think she understood what I'd said—humans aren't really intelligent enough to understand complex speech—but she understood my meaning, and that was all that mattered. We were moving on, just the two of us.

"Wait!" Strawman hollered as he scampered over. He hurdled over my head and landed next to Dorothy. "Don't go without me."

"I'm coming, too," Metal Man said. His footsteps thundered behind me like a booming metal drum. "But where's the little dog? I don't want to step on him."

"I'm here," I barked in annoyance. I'm not that little. He could see me if he slowed down long enough to look.

"Don't leave me alone with that chipmunk!" Big Cat yowled. He caught up to Dorothy in two great bounding leaps. I have to admit, it looked pretty impressive. But then he wrapped his tail around his arm and started to bite his claws, so the impressive effect wore off right away. What a big baby.

Anyway, here we were, all five of us marching down the brick road to find a mysterious lizard who was supposed to feed porridge to the lion and help us get home. And give the straw guy a drain or a crane or maybe a brain. Actually, all four of them needed a brain, or at least they needed to make better use of the ones they had.

And the metal guy needed something, too. Maybe something to fill up his insides so he wouldn't make so much noise when he bumped into things. We could probably stuff the straw guy inside the metal guy, and then I'd only have two of these clowns to deal with instead of three.

As we walked, the overgrown kitten kept looking over at me, as if he were afraid I might bite his ankle.

I have better manners than that. Since Dorothy accepted him, I had to accept him, too.

But that didn't mean I had to like him.

The next time he looked down at me, I growled, and he yelped and ran forward. Yep, he was afraid of me. I felt pretty good about that. If he understood I could take him out any time I wanted, we would get along just fine.

Chapter 8

"*W*ahhhhhhhhhhhhhhhhh!*" A horrible wailing noise ripped through the air.

What the...?

I looked around. The painful noise was so loud and so sudden and so...well, echo-y. It just kept going. It sounded like it was coming from one of the weirdos in our strange little posse, but none of them had their mouths open.

But soon Metal Man opened his mouth, and the noise grew louder, so I figured the wailing cry had just been echoing around his hollow metal insides. Tears gushed out of his eyes and streamed down his face in a torrent.

"What's wrong?" I barked in desperation. It may have looked like I was concerned for him, but really, I was afraid he would let out another loud cry and my sensitive ears just couldn't handle the strain.

With his joints creaking in protest, he bent down and scooped up a beetle in the palm of his shiny hand. Then he let loose another wail, and it took me a while to recover from that. When I opened my eyes again,

Metal Man was still blubbering like a puppy on his first night away from the litter.

The beetle didn't look too happy, either. It was, in fact, dead. And I think that was why Metal Man was crying. He had killed it.

I felt sorry for him. Well, for both of them, actually. I felt sorry for the beetle because he was just minding his own business and then probably thought "Hey, look at that big shiny metal thing over my hea—" And boom—that was it for him. I felt sorry for Metal Man because he was a mess. He moaned and wailed. Tears ran in rivers down his cheeks, spilling down his neck and over his big empty ham can of a chest. They dribbled down the joints in his shoulders and down onto his arms.

He was starting to rust.

Dorothy dried his tears with a dishtowel; then, she and the overgrown cat tried to pull him up and get him to walk. But he was stuck in a bent-over position with his head pointed down and couldn't move too well.

"He needs that can of whatever you used on him before," I barked to Dorothy. "You know, the can that wasn't food."

She just pushed me away.

I tried to explain the situation to Big Cat.

"There's a can of stuff that smells like tractor," I barked.

He wouldn't listen, either. So, I went over to Strawman.

"Get that can of stuff from before."

He acted like he didn't even see me. But he reached into Dorothy's basket and found the can we needed.

I think I must be having a good influence on Strawman. He's growing smarter just by watching my intelligent behavior.

When they put the stuff from the can on Metal Man, he loosened up, just like before. But he walked very slowly, as if he were still rusty.

"I don't want to step on anything else," he explained.

It was a great goal, but he was moving so slowly the rest of us were likely to start rusting, and we weren't even made of metal. Eventually, Strawman got him to speed up by telling him Dorothy was getting cold and needed to keep moving to stay warm.

When we got ready to camp that night, I ran around barking and snapping at the grass.

"Watch out," I warned. "You don't want to get stepped on by clumsy people with big feet." I wasn't at all sure any of the beetles or other bugs could understand me, but I figured it was worth a try.

"Bblubbluthanks!" a tiny voice answered from a tuft of clover. It was such a soft voice, and so hard to understand I thought I'd imagined it.

"Hey," I called, to see if there really was something to talk to. "Is someone there? Where are we? What is this strange land?"

I heard this faint answer that sounded like "Ozzzzzzzzzzzzzzzz." That seemed like just a regular insect noise to me, so I guess I must have a imagined the "thanks" earlier. I was so desperate for someone to talk to I was hearing voices in the grass. Not good.

But even if they hadn't understood me, the bugs stayed away, so we had no more crying episodes from Metal Man. After all, sometime the stuff in that can will run out, and then if he cries, he'll just be stuck.

It was really dark by this time. The edges of the road were crumbly and uneven, and the bricks were covered with matted leaves, as if no one had paid attention to this stretch of the road for a very long time. We piled some leaves to sit on, and Dorothy handed me a piece of dry bread. It was tasteless, but at least it was people food.

Big Cat left, supposedly to hunt for his dinner. He tried to make us think he was a really fierce hunter, but I think I smelled French fries on his breath when he came back, so he probably just found a restaurant and scared someone into giving him their food.

Anyway, since Strawman and Metal Man don't eat, at least we don't have to share with them.

When we were in Kansas, Dorothy always talked to me as we lay cuddled in the dark. But tonight, except for feeding me and scolding me when I growled at Big Cat for not bringing me a hamburger, she seemed to ignore my existence. Sometimes, I thought she wished I wasn't even here.

I had a hard time falling asleep that night. I might have even cried a little, but don't tell anyone.

Chapter 9

The next morning, once we all finally managed to wake Big Cat and get started, we didn't get very far. Actually, we almost went *too* far. The road kind of disappeared into a great ditch so deep even the biggest dog couldn't have dug it in a million years.

It was a little foggy that morning, and we were all thinking about what we'd had (or didn't have) for breakfast, so if Strawman hadn't held out his arms to stop them, Dorothy and Big Cat would have plunged over the edge.

"Thank you," Dorothy gushed. "You saved us."

"Wow!" Big Cat exclaimed. "I can't believe I didn't see that huge—hey, the sun's trying to come out. Do you think my back will get sunburned?"

Metal Man paused for a moment, like he was seriously considering it. Then he shook his head.

"I think you're good. But how are we going to cross this chasm?"

I couldn't even smell the bottom of that ditch, it was so deep. Everyone looked around, trying to figure out how to get across it. It was too steep to climb down—even a monkey probably couldn't manage it.

He'd need wings or something. And whoever heard of a monkey with wings?

"I've got this," Big Cat announced calmly. Apparently, he thought he had wings, because he crouched and sprang up in a great leap across the ditch.

Well, that's the end of him, I thought gleefully.

But it wasn't. He landed safely on the other side with a big grin on his shaggy face.

He jumped back over to our side, and Strawman climbed onto his back, getting tangled in the cat's matted fur. The Big Cat made another leap to carry him across. And then he did the same with Metal Man.

Oh, no. No way.

Dorothy scooped me up in her arms, and I think she was planning to carry me across on the cat's back. I'd rather jump myself.

I tried to get away, but she held me tight by the collar, which is cheating because none of the rest of them had to wear a collar. Anyway, when the cat came back, she climbed on.

The cat's back smelled even worse than his feet, which is usually the only part of him I can smell, since he's so much bigger than me. The big smelly cat crouched and then, without warning, leapt into the air. We went up—a lot higher than necessary, I thought—and for a while it didn't seem like we would ever touch the ground again. The sensation made me dizzy, and I felt like I was going to barf all over Dorothy's lap. I had to get away. So, I took a deep breath and jumped off, since by that time we were close enough for me to reach the ground.

Well, we would have been close enough if the cat hadn't tried to show off by jumping so high. We weren't as close as I'd thought, so only my front paws reached the other side. The rest of me was left dangling in the air. I would have been really embarrassed if I hadn't been so scared.

"Help me!" I barked frantically. I scratched at the rocks and dirt, trying to get a foothold, but everything just crumbled and fell to the bottom of the chasm. At least, I think that's where they fell. I never heard anything land—it was that deep.

Just when I thought I would lose my grip and fall down through the center of the Earth and out the other side, the Metal Man reached down and pulled me to safety.

But safety wasn't safe for long.

Grrrlllllfff.
Rrrghh fffrrraaarrrwwwggg.

We weren't too far into the woods on the other side of the chasm when I heard these weird growling noises. The trees were so close together and the fog was so dense we could see only a few feet around us, so I couldn't tell what was making that noise. It didn't sound friendly. Or I should say, *they* didn't sound friendly, because whatever made the noise, it sounded like there was more than one. At first, I was the only one who seemed to notice.

Then they got louder.

Ggssaarrrassnnb ppprrrsseeaafff

Which meant they were closer.

Big Cat stopped and grabbed his tail with both hands.

"W-what was that?" he asked in a shaky voice.

"I've been woods a long time," Metal Man said slowly, "and I've never heard a sound like it."

"It sounds big, maybe as big as him." Strawman pointed at Big Cat.

"As big as me?" Big Cat asked skeptically. "D'ye really think so? I think it's something a little smaller because my roar is much—"

"Look, guys," I barked, "it doesn't matter exactly how big it is. It's something we don't want to meet. So, let's run."

Of course, since they couldn't understand me, they all just stood around waiting for whatever it was to attack us.

Grrraallphhhggg.

Big Cat listened closely for a moment.

"I think it might be almost as big as me, but maybe not quite."

I wasn't going to wait around for the end of this debate. I took off running and hoped the others would either follow me or prove to be such a filling meal for the growling monsters they wouldn't need to catch me for dessert.

The bricks were crumbly and uneven and slippery with moss. I finally decided it would be faster to run next to the road. But there I had to fight my way through piles of decaying leaves. The growling and snuffling of the creatures grew louder, but not too much, so I hoped we might still be able to get away

Then we came to another enormous ditch. This one was so wide even Big Cat couldn't jump across.

The smell of fear hung heavy in the air, and I am ashamed to admit that some of it came from me. Probably most of it came from me. I'd almost died trying to cross the last chasm, and here was an even bigger one; and we couldn't stay where we were because those growling things were about to catch up to us.

Strawman jabbered loudly to Metal Man, but I was so scared, I couldn't focus on what he was saying.

"Something tree something something," he hollered.

"This is no time to talk," I barked. "This is a time to panic."

But Strawman kept pointing and talking. And then Metal Man took his axe and started whacking at one of the big trees near the edge of the ditch.

"This is no time to work," I barked. "This is a time to panic."

After a few minutes, Big Cat jumped up and started to push against the tree trunk.

"This is no time to exercise," I barked. I was going to say it was time to panic, but the growling had grown so much louder I think we had passed panic.

It was time to be eaten.

Grrrrraawwwllff.

Out of the fog came two enormous black creatures with heads like tigers and bodies like bears and a smell like the neighbor with the pitchfork. The horrible creatures advanced slowly, their hideous teeth bared and the growling more intense with each passing second.

But instead of cowering in fright, Big Cat gave one final mighty push against the tree, toppling it forward so that it crashed down with the top of its trunk on the other side of the chasm, creating a bridge.

"*Go!*" Strawman yelled, pushing us all out onto the tree trunk.

I ran as fast as my legs could carry me. And so did everyone else, including those black tiger-bear things.

When we reached the other side, Strawman pointed to the place where the tree trunk rested on the edge of the chasm.

"Okay, now cut it off," he ordered.

With a few swift strokes of the axe, Metal Man chopped it through and our bridge collapsed, taking those two nasty black creatures down to the bottom of the gorge. I listened to see if I could hear them splat at the bottom, but I never heard anything—as far as I know, they might have gone straight through the planet and fallen out the other side.

The acrid, painful smell of fear began to subside. We were safe, but who knew for how long?

I would trade every pork chop in the universe for the chance to be back in Kansas again, where there were no big black tiger-bears and all the ditches were narrow enough for me to jump over on my own.

The fields ahead of us looked perfectly safe.

Chapter 10

We were all tired, but we had to keep walking. I was getting really sick of trees. They seemed to close in on all sides, so we could never see more than about two feet ahead of us. Well, maybe three feet.

After we'd crossed that last big ditch, though, I noticed the trees seemed to be getting farther apart. They were a little shorter, too, I think. I could see leaves now instead of just big dark branches stretching densely overhead.

After a while, I was certain. The trees *were* farther apart. I could see grass ahead. We were coming out of the woods!

I ran down the hate-able brick road as fast as lightning, headed for the field of grass and weeds and those tall sticks with petals on top that Dorothy likes to smell. I think they're called flavors or flowers or something like that.

"Toto, come back!" Dorothy yelled. She sounded really scared.

"Don't worry!" I barked. "We have nothing to be afraid of over there." There were no big scary tiger-bear things out in that field, I just knew it.

Suddenly, though, I smelled salty water. I slowed down. That wasn't dew on the grass or rainwater. It smelled like Auntem was getting ready to cook fish. But she wasn't here, and there weren't any fish in that field.

Dorothy caught up with me and scooped me up into her arms. I licked her cheek. As she held me tight, I thought maybe she *hadn't* forgotten all about me after all. It almost felt like the old days back on the farm where it was just the two of us.

Then the straw guy ruined everything by jabbering.

"Now we've got something else to cross."

Dorothy looked at him instead of me.

"What should we do?"

"Oh, this truly sucks." Big Cat stuck his thumb in his mouth and twisted a tuft of fur around his other paw. He suddenly reeked with the smell of fear.

I crawled up toward Dorothy's shoulder, and soon I could see what they were talking about.

Yikes!

That saltwater smell was coming from a giant bathtub. The water was in constant motion, as if some giant creature were taking a bath at one end and pushing the water toward the other end. It was so big, I couldn't see either end of the tub. It was the most frightening thing I could ever imagine. An endless bath.

Other than Big Cat, though, no one else seemed too scared by it.

"I think if we make a something we can float across," Strawman said as he stared out over the expanse of rushing water.

"I'll something the wood," Metal Man offered, holding up his axe.

Well, at least I knew this plan involved chopping.

Metal Man started to cut down trees, but there weren't any long enough to use to cross the hugenormous bathtub the way we had crossed the giant ditch. The bathtub might not be as deep, but it was a lot wider.

Metal Man cut many trees, and after a while, the rhythmic chopping sound made me sleepy. As I settled down to keep watch for tiger-bears, I was dimly aware that Strawman and Big Cat had started tying the tree trunks together with ground ivy. Dorothy was picking berries from some bushes by the water.

It was important for me to keep low and stay very still as I watched for tiger-bears so I would see them before they saw me. In fact, I had to stay so still it probably looked like I was asleep, but I wasn't.

Well, maybe right at the end, for just a second.

The next thing I knew, Dorothy was holding me in her arms. A water smell hit me like egg in the face. She was going to give me a bath!

I wriggled out of her arms and jumped to freedom, but I didn't get very far. We were all on a floor of logs that was floating in the giant bathtub. I could only run a few steps before I had to stop to keep from falling into the evil water.

Strawman used a pole to push us across the water.

"Stay back," I barked as a warning to the water. "If you try to wash us, I'll pee in you and make you turn dark and smelly."

I went around and repeated this warning on all sides, to make sure all the water heard it.

My constant barking was working, but the others didn't understand what I was doing.

"Toto, hush!" Dorothy repeated over and over. She didn't understand. If I stopped barking, they all would have been cleaned against their wishes.

Nobody even thanked me.

As soon as we reached the other side, I jumped onto the grassy bank and ran as far away from that bathtub as I could.

"Toto!" Dorothy called in a very annoyed tone. "Come here."

I hesitated, but not for very long. She is my pet girl, after all, and I couldn't leave her all alone with the three freaks. So, I turned around and ran back over to her.

"Where is the (whatever that word was) brick road?" Strawman asked, looking around.

"I don't know," Metal Man answered. He held up his axe to shield his eyes from the sun as he looked in each direction.

Big Cat stretched up on the tips of his paws.

"That must be it over—hey, those flowers smell good." He dashed over to a bed of tall flowers, bent down and inhaled deeply.

I didn't really care whether we found the brick road again or not. I was getting really tired of those bricks, and that road seemed to lead to nothing but trouble. The fields ahead of us looked perfectly safe, nothing but grass and flowers, with no trees to hide bears or giant ditches. I didn't agree with Big Cat—I didn't think the flowers smelled good. I actually thought they smelled icky. Really icky, like there was something wrong with them, like it would make you barf if you ate them.

But I didn't think I really would barf. I was too tired to barf. I was suddenly too tired to stand. It was way past time for my nap. It was even past time for Dorothy's nap, and she never takes naps.

It was naptime for everyone. We all lay down to rest. The last thing I remember was Metal Man crying, but I didn't know why.

Chapter 11

We were back in Kansas again. I don't know how it happened, but there was no mistaking the warm spot on the floor at the foot of Dorothy's bed or the smell of bacon cooking in the kitchen. I could even hear pop-corn popping—it was going to be a feast. The popcorn kernels must have been unusually large. They popped with a real bang.

Outside, Unclehenry must have been running a sprinkler, because I could feel drops of water coming in through the window. Like the popcorn, the drops of water were super-big. I was starting to feel like I'd been tricked into taking a shower.

I crawled under Dorothy's bed, but it was even wet under there. Then the bed roared. The mattress opened up a great, enormous mouth and tried to eat me. The popcorn had become so huge and loud the floor was shaking with each pop. I was so scared I was covered with sweat.

Wait a minute, dogs only sweat through their feet. Why was I so wet?

I opened my eyes, and the giant hungry mattress was gone. In its place was a big guy made of metal and another big guy stuffed with straw. Neither of them seemed to want to eat me, so I felt much better. But I was still wet.

It was drizzling rain. A flash of lightning whipped across the sky, followed by a great booming roar of thunder. So, it wasn't popcorn after all. No bacon, either. I must have dreamed it all.

And the worst part was that we weren't back at home. We were still in the weird place with bizarre people made out of metal and straw.

At least Dorothy was with me. She sat up and rubbed her eyes. She started talking to Strawman and Metal Man, but she looked at *me* and reached over to rub behind my ears. I love it when she does that.

Soon, the rain stopped, but I didn't get up to shake the water off from my fur until after Dorothy had tired of petting me.

A great roaring yawn sounded at my side. Big Cat grimaced as he wiped water out of his eyes. I don't think he liked getting a shower any more than I did.

The last thing I remembered, before the dream of popcorn and bacon, was a field of smelly flowers. Now we were in a field of corn—still growing, not popping. I could barely see the flowers in the distance. Had we sleepwalked all this way? Or had someone carried us away from the smelly flowers? Strawman and Metal Man were the only ones who hadn't gotten sleepy, so they must have.

I wondered if I should bark a "thank you" to them for moving us. If it hadn't been for them, we might have stayed sleeping in that field forever. The icky smell from the flowers must have been poison of some kind.

I had to admit, the straw guy and the metal man could be useful. So, maybe I *should* thank them.

Instead, I decided I wouldn't try to bite their ankles anymore.

By now, the rain had stopped for good, and the sun started to peek through the clouds. After we shook off most of the water, Dorothy and the other three started to jabber and point in every direction.

"Do you see the mellow brick road?" Dorothy asked.

"I think it must be that way," Strawman replied, pointing toward the south.

Metal Man opened his mouth like he was going to say something, but then it just stayed open, and no real words came out.

"Aaahhh," he said, sounding a little desperate.

"I think he needs that stuff in the can," I barked. "He's rusted from the rain."

"Toto's hungry," Big Cat announced. "I understand dogs."

"No, you don't," I barked with contempt. "I mean, yes, I am hungry, but I wasn't talking about it or anything." For that matter, I hadn't been thinking about it, either, until he mentioned it, stupid feline.

"Well, we don't have any food," Dorothy announced. "We need to find the hello brick road. I think we should go that way." She pointed to the field of flowers. "Strawman thinks we should go that way." She pointed to fields of grass in the opposite direction. "And Metal Man seems to have no idea."

"No," I barked, "he just can't tell you his idea because his mouth is rusted shut. Give him the stuff from the can."

"What do you think?" Dorothy asked Big Cat.

He leaned around in every direction before responding.

"I think the road is—do I smell popcorn?"

"No," I barked. "I thought the same thing. But it's just corn growing in the fields. It's not ready to eat yet."

I wanted to go back to Kansas so bad, but nothing here smelled even vaguely like the dry hard earth and plains of windswept grass of the prairie. How would we ever find our way home? There were no familiar scents at all. All I could smell was the strange spongy grass, the green ears of corn in the fields, the faint odors of brick dust and those icky flowers.

Brick? I could smell brick! I could find the road again by the smell.

Following the smell, I headed off through the corn stalks, barking for the others to follow.

"Come on, guys, I know the way!"

"Toto, come back," Dorothy called.

I kept going. The scent of brick dust was damp—I could only smell the bricks because of the rain. But the rain had stopped, so the bricks would dry out, and then I might not be able to track the scent.

"Toto!" Dorothy yelled again. Now she sounded angry.

I kept running. Soon, I heard the sound of someone crunching and swishing through the cornstalks behind me. She, and maybe the others, were following me. That made me happy, and gave me energy to run even faster. The scent was growing stronger, but it was changing, too. Drying out.

I kept going, hoping the others would stay with me. It was getting harder to run through the mud, since the gloppy muck clung to my paws, making them heavier and heavier with each step. I would make a big mess on Auntem's clean floor, that was for sure. But if we didn't figure out a way to get home, I might never see that floor again. That thought kept me going.

All of a sudden, I realized I could hear more than Dorothy stumbling through the corn behind me. I heard horses' hooves on something hard.

Bricks?

Probably.

I ran toward the sound. I saw a break in the cornstalks. An open space where a road might be.

The brick road. I had found it! Hurrah!

I climbed up to the bricks and lay down to rest while I waited for the others to catch up. I could see a horse coming toward me. And I could see some tall things way in the distance. They weren't shaped like trees. They were too regular— like tall barns, reflecting sunlight onto the fields around. Maybe it was a city of horses.

I wished it was a city of pigs because I hadn't had a good pork chop in ages.

When Dorothy and the others finally caught up to me, I waited for her to pet me and offer me the rest of the bread from her basket. Instead, they all pointed toward the giant barns and started hugging each other.

"We did it!" Dorothy yelled joyously.

Strawman did a little wriggly dance.

"We found the something city," he sang.

They acted as if they'd found it themselves. I was so mad, I almost took a bite out of the Metal Man's ankle as he stepped past me.

Then I remembered that (1) I had vowed not to bite him anymore in gratitude for carrying us away from the flowers and (2) he *was* made of metal, so if I bit him it would really hurt—me.

They started joyously skipping down the brick road toward the giant shiny barns. I followed. Not skipping.

As we got closer, we could see that the barns were enclosed by a wall made of horse blankets. Or at least, they looked like blankets from a distance. When we got close, we could tell the wall was a lot harder, made of something that looked like dried oatmeal but smelled like a mixture of leather and stone. I couldn't dig under it without a lot of tunneling, and we couldn't see any way around it. None of us was very good at climbing, either.

We needed a gate.

Fortunately, after walking around a little, we spotted one, or at least, what we hoped was one. It really looked like a pie. A big metal pie on its side. It was round. It didn't have a crust. Okay, it really didn't look that much like a pie, I was just hungry. It smelled like Metal Man, so I guess if it was a pie, it would taste about as good as biting his ankle—not that I was stupid enough to try that.

"Open up!" I barked at the gate, hoping it would listen and open.

It didn't.

Dorothy and the others started talking to it, too. Or maybe they were talking to each other. I couldn't tell, and it didn't much matter because the pie gate remained closed. I couldn't see a doorknob or a latch or anything. How did people get through the wall to the other side?

Did people get through the wall to the other side?

And, of course, this brought up the whole question of why *we* wanted to get through the wall to the other side. I don't know about the others, but my answer had a lot to do with food. A big place surrounded by a wall that looked like oatmeal with a gate shaped like a pie had to have food in it somewhere.

I went close to the gate to sniff for food on the other side. At first, I smelled nothing but rust. I sniffed harder. I sniffed so hard my nose squeaked and started to melt into the gate.

That was creepy. Oh, no, wait. The gate was just pushing open a little bit when I nudged it. The squeaking noise came from the hinges, not my nose. The gate wasn't even closed all the way, much less locked! But it was too heavy for me to push open on my own.

"Hey, guys," I barked. "It's not locked! Help me open it."

Strawman noticed first, but he didn't have much more luck pushing on it than I did, so he got Metal Man to help.

As the big iron pie pan of a gate swung open, I thought about what might be waiting on the other side. Pork chops, mashed potatoes, green beans—I could smell them all.

And fur. I could smell fur, too.

What if the pork chops and green beans were being cooked by some of the those big black tiger-bear things that had chased us earlier? We might be walking right onto their next menu.

But it was too late now. The gate was open. And if I didn't want to get left outside, I would have to follow the others inside.

Chapter 12

Inside was really still outside, since the open sky was overhead, but it felt very different. Most noticeable was how bright it was. Tall buildings stretched up on all sides, but it was hard to look at them because of the way they glistened and sparkled in the sunlight. The longer we stood there by the gate, the brighter it got, and soon I had to squeeze my eyes shut to block out the glare.

"I can't see!" Dorothy exclaimed. "It's too bright."

"Put your tail over your eyes," Big Cat suggested. "The long strands of hair help block the light."

I pointed out the problem with this brilliant plan. "Dorothy can't do that, you brainasaurus-not," I barked. "Her tail is stuck under her dress."

"What's all this, then?" a gruff voice asked. It was a man's voice, like Unclehenry's but not as deep, so I wondered if it might be one of those people-who-can't-quite-reach things. But even if he was smaller than Unclehenry, he was still probably a lot bigger than me, and he sounded mean and he might have a pitch-fork. I tried to hide behind Dorothy, but since I couldn't see, I couldn't tell if I was hiding behind her or standing in front of her. At least, it was comforting to have her smell close to me.

"You must put these on," the man with the gruff voice ordered.

What was he ordering us to put on? Leashes? Handcuffs? The way I see it, those are things someone else is supposed to force on you. You don't willingly lock yourself into them.

"Oh, that's much better," Dorothy said with relief.

"Thank you," Metal Man said gratefully. "I was so afraid I might step on something while my eyes were closed."

All at once, someone who did not smell like Dorothy lifted me into the air. Before I could decide whether to bite or wriggle free, the someone slipped something behind my ears and across my nose.

Forgetting the painful light for a moment, I opened my eyes to see what was on my face. It was a pair of glasses, like Auntem wore when she was reading the book she read before she cooked dinner, but the glass part was darker than the glass in Auntem's glasses. When I looked through the darkened glass, I could see without pain.

The problem was that, because the glasses were hooked over my ears and my ears are on top of my head, I could only look straight down. I had a nice comfortable view of the ground, but if I wanted to look at anything else, I still had to squint and put up with a lot of pain.

A quick glance at the others showed they had been given dark glasses, too, but theirs fit better than mine did. Except for Big Cat—his eyes were so far apart the glasses really didn't come anywhere near to covering them. So, he had to squint, too.

Since I had to keep my eyes nearly shut, I wanted to snuggle with Dorothy and take a nap. Instead, I had to walk because everyone else wanted to explore this strange bright city that was protected by that big wall.

Was the wall designed to keep the people of the city in, like the fence at our farm that kept the cows from trampling the neighbor's flowers? Or was the wall designed to keep something outside from getting inside? Maybe something capable of attacking.

Like me.

"Right, then," the man with the gruff voice announced. "Let's go." He set off with a funny little march step.

The city was full of buildings that were twice as tall as our house in Kansas. They were all clustered close together, so there was no room for a chicken coop or even a doghouse between them. Sparkly stones glittered everywhere.

As we walked down streets made of shiny bricks, the people who lived in the city pointed and whispered to each other. They were almost as tall as people back in Kansas, but they smelled more like plants.

"I'm taking you to the lizard," our gruff-voiced guide told Dorothy. "Our leader will want to know why you're here."

"We've come to see the lizard to get some brains." she answered.

He stopped and looked at us. "All of you?"

"Well, no," Dorothy explained. "Strawman is the only one who wants brains."

"I want *my* brains," Big Cat corrected her. "I just don't happen to need any more of them."

"He needs porridge," Metal Man added. "Although you'd never know it from the rude way he just interrupted Dorothy."

"And *he* needs a muzzle," Big Cat growled. "But he's asking for a cart instead."

As far as I was concerned, the Big Cat needed a muzzle, too. At least I now knew for certain the

Strawman was looking for intelligence rather than transportation.

"That's all well and good," our gruff-voiced guide said, nodding, "but what do you want, Miss?" He turned to Dorothy.

"I want to go home."

His face cracked into a smile. "Well, unless you live here, you're not going to find what you want in this place." He sniggered at his own weak joke.

Instead of laughing with him, however, Dorothy began to sniff. Her eyes were all watery with unshed tears.

So were mine. The guide hadn't asked what I wanted.

"I want a pork chop," I barked, hoping to get his attention. It had been a long time since I'd eaten anything worth eating.

"Toto wants to go home, too," Dorothy said.

Well, yes, I did want that. But first things first.

"Very well, very well, see what the lizard says," our guide said as he started to march forward again.

I sighed. I guess I would have to settle for some of the porridge the lizard would give to Big Cat.

I didn't see much of the city during our walk, other than the street. Little bugs that reminded me of the potato bugs back home scurried along between the bricks, singing songs that, as far as I could tell, had nothing to do with potatoes. I couldn't understand them perfectly, but they spoke much better than people do.

After watching them for a while, I started to like the little guys. Once, when I saw one of them walking on top of the bricks instead of in between, I blew him off the road to keep him from being squashed by the Metal Man's heavy feet.

"Hey!" the bug squeaked indignantly. "Why'd ya do that?"

"You might have gotten stepped on," I barked.

"Oh." The bug looked up—way up—at the metal man and the others walking by. "*Uuhbndgd*! Thanks!" The bug saluted me with his antennae before scurrying back down between the bricks.

It took me a moment to realize what had just happened. I had understood him quite clearly.

And he understood me!

"Wait," I yipped, hoping to learn more about this place. "Come back." But he was gone.

It was so exciting to have a friend to talk to. I decided to name him Bob. Or maybe Dave or Bill.

While I was still thinking about which name to use, everyone stopped, and I ran into the back of Dorothy's shiny witch shoe.

"Wait here while I something something," our guide ordered as he continued on by himself.

I looked up to discover we were stopped in front of a big tall building, bigger and taller than all of the others. It was as big as the Cow Palace at the State Fair, but I didn't smell any cows, only those people who smelled like green plants. There was a smell of pork chops and hamburger and sweaty socks coming from the building, too. But something wasn't quite right, as if the pork chops were very old or the socks had been washed.

Two of the men who smelled like plants stood guard outside the enormous door to what I started to think of as "the People Palace." The guards held sharp metal sticks, like pitchforks with only one tine. Were they trying to keep us outside?

Or trying to keep something dangerous locked inside?

Before I could begin to imagine what dangerous thing might be locked inside the People Palace, our guide came back, opened the door and let us enter. Inside, it wasn't as bright, and I could see without looking through the glasses, so I shook them off and let them clatter to the floor.

Once our eyes adjusted to the dimmer light, we saw another door, covered with sparkling stones. It was big enough to drive a tractor through. More than that—it was big enough to drive about five tractors through all stacked on top of one another. Whatever was behind that door was very tall and smelled like moldy pork chops.

I wanted to cry because they had let the pork chops go bad. Well, they didn't really smell completely bad. It was like you might be able to eat them, but they'd make you feel sick.

Naturally, we all started to walk toward this giant door, but then another set of guards lowered their pitchforks at us.

"No one is permitted to see the lizard without his orders," the one closest to us proclaimed.

"You have to wait with the others," the other one added.

It wasn't until then that I noticed the other people sitting on cushioned benches that lined the cavernous room. Lots of people. They smelled like the first lettuces in a spring garden and were dressed like they were going to see a dead person put into the ground. Did all these people want to get in to see the lizard, too? Even if he only had spoiled pork chops to offer?

Dorothy, Strawman, Metal Man and Big Cat all started talking at once.

"I have the something shoes of the something something of the East," Dorothy announced.

"She was told to come here," Strawman contended.

"Please?" Metal Man asked. "She deserves to see the lizard."

"You can't make us wait outside," Big Cat insisted. "I might get sunburned."

Dorothy took off one of her shiny shoes to hand to the guard, and he opened the door and carried it away. As he passed through the doorway, we all looked closely but couldn't see anything on the other side, only a vast dark space.

While the guard was gone, I sniffed Dorothy's foot to see if her sock smelled as weird as the shoe, but it just smelled like Dorothy, which was okay. Everything in this city was so shiny and glittery, maybe they used sparkles like money and maybe Dorothy had to use her fancy shoe to pay to get into the next room, like paying to get into the Cow Palace to see the prize-winning bulls.

So, what were we paying to see at the People Palace? I didn't think I'd ever seen a person worth giving a prize to.

After a while, the guard came back with Dorothy's shoe. He opened the door and gestured for her to step inside, but he held his pitchfork up to keep the others from following. He couldn't stop me, though, because I'm too fast. (Okay, and being short doesn't hurt, either). I scurried after her through the doorway into the darkness beyond.

Chapter 13

The door slammed behind us with an ominous thud. I couldn't smell the pork chops so much anymore, as if the aroma had blown away, even though the air in the room was completely still. As we walked forward, our movement caused fabric panels along the wall to rustle, as if nothing had moved in this room for a very long time and even the walls wanted to talk about it.

When my eyes had adjusted to the dark, I saw the prize-winning person who was on display in the People Palace, sitting in a giant chair. He was big, alright, like the bulls and pigs you see at the State Fair, but the prize-winning person was really deformed. He had an enormous pale head and a very small body. So small you could hardly see it.

We decided to go closer. Okay, *Dorothy* decided to go closer, and I decided I didn't want to get left behind in the strange place. Then, I realized the prize-winning person had no body at all. Just a giant head. No wonder they kept the place so dark.

The head opened its mouth and words came out— at least I assume they were real words, I didn't understand all of them because he talked like a person.

"I am the something lizard," he announced in a booming voice. "Who are you, and why did you come to see me?"

Wait a minute. *This* was the lizard we had traveled all this way to see? He didn't have smooth scales and an elegant long tail. He didn't even have a body. He was just a big fat head!

Dorothy started to shake, and the smell of fear poured off her in waves.

"Knock it off, Fathead," I barked. "You have no right to scare my girl!"

The head laughed. Either he hadn't understood me, or he didn't mind at all that I'd called him "fathead."

I have to admit it was probably that he hadn't understood me.

"Where did you get the something shoes?" he asked.

Dorothy had to take a few deep breaths before she was able to answer. "F-From the something ditch of the East," she said finally.

That confused me for a second. She'd gotten the shoes from a dead creature underneath our house, but the ground had been pretty flat—no ditch that I could remember.

Then I realized Dorothy must have been making up an answer to trick the Fathead.

He asked her more questions about the ditch, and Dorothy shook her head and said she really didn't know, so I guess she had already run out of made-up answers. She should have asked me—I know a lot more about ditches than she does.

But she didn't, so I ignored their babble and started to sniff around the room, hoping to find the porridge Big Cat had come for. There wasn't much to smell, though. The big fat head in the chair had no smell at all, like it wasn't even there. Like a shadow.

But there was so little light, there couldn't be any shadows.

Then, suddenly, there was a flash of light with a picture of a face just next to the giant chair. It was a female human's face—sort of. Really ugly and old, like the neighbor back in Kansas with the pitchfork. But even worse—as if the ugly old face had been buried in the ground for a while and started to rot.

The face faded away, and with another flash, it was replaced by a picture of a dark stone silo surrounded by water. Finally, there was a picture of something else. Something that looked like a stick.

Did Fathead want Dorothy to throw a stick at the silo? Or at the ugly face? Did the ugly face have a body, or was it just a head, like Fathead?

Maybe Dorothy would throw the stick and the ugly face would have to pick it up, like I always had to do back in Kansas.

Other possibilities flashed through my head.

He could turn *us* into ugly faces.

Or feed us to the ugly face.

Make us look ugly.

Ask us to take the ugly face out to dinner (this was really just wishful thinking on my part).

Take the ugly face back to Kansas and throw sticks for her to pick up.

Or throw sticks in the water around the silo for the ugly face to fetch.

He might want us to give the ugly face a bath in all that water.

Or worst of all—make us to go the stone silo to get a bath ourselves.

Before I could come up with an answer that made much sense, Fathead commanded in a booming voice, "Before I help you get home, you must bring me the something of the ditch of the West."

Someone needed to teach this guy how to use visual aids properly with his speeches. He showed us pictures of an ugly face, a silo and a stick and talked about a ditch in the west. How about a picture of a ditch? And he could have used a setting sun to demonstrate west. I'd give him a D-minus for his random use of pictures.

But apparently Dorothy understood him, even with his mismatched visual aids. She started crying.

"I'd probably have to kill her to get it," she said.

That was enough.

I ran up to the chair, growling and snapping at the chair rungs.

"You can't scare my girl, Fathead!" I barked. "You don't even have any legs to chase her. What are you going to do, roll over us?"

I jumped up and tried to bite the Fathead, but unfortunately, I can't jump real high due to an old chicken-chasing injury.

"Toto, come back," Dorothy called in a tearful voice.

For a moment, I was torn between my duty to protect her and my desire to obey and make her happy. I decided to make her happy, and rushed over to lick her ankles. She scooped me into her arms, cuddling me close and wiping her tears on my hair. At least her nose wasn't running. Yet.

I hated the Fathead for making my girl cry. Crying means she's really unhappy. And wet.

She turned and walked slowly back to the door with me in her arms. By the time we got there, I felt like I'd been caught in a thundersnot storm. She shook her head sadly at Strawman but couldn't manage to talk to him as we came out.

"You go next," Big Cat waved his tail at Strawman.

"There's no fire, is there?" Strawman asked Dorothy.

She shook her head no.

He looked fearfully at the giant door ahead of him. "That's the only thing I'm really afraid of. Fire."

"Well," Big Cat drawled, "there's no fire here, and you're still afraid. Your legs are shaking like jelly."

"Oh, yeah?" Strawman spun around to face him. "Well, you're so scared you've already chewed off half the fur on your tail."

"I've been trimming it," Big Cat insisted. "It was uneven."

"Would you just get in there before I drown!" I barked.

Okay, so he couldn't understand me. At least my barking got him to stop arguing and go in. He came out a few minutes later shaking his head sadly as if he did not know what to do.

"You're next," he said to Metal Man.

"O-Okay," he answered. His arms and legs rattled so much as he walked in I wondered if he might shake himself all to pieces, and if he did, whether anyone would bother to tell us or if we'd just wait all day while Dorothy drowned us all in her tears.

"Don't cry, Dorothy," Strawman said gently. "If you stop crying, I'll tell you something funny."

She sniffed. "Okay, tell me."

"The lizard told me to kill the something ditch of the West." He gave a mirthless laugh. "Me! I couldn't even manage to scare a few birds."

Dorothy started in surprise. "He told me to kill the ditch, too."

"You must have misunderstood him," I barked. "You can't kill a ditch. But you can pee in it and make it smell bad. He probably told you to *fill* the ditch."

Then Metal Man came out.

"At least you have an axe," Strawman said. "Did he tell you to kill the ditch, too?"

"*Fill* the ditch, you crazy can," I barked. "He wants you to fill it, not kill it."

He acted like he hadn't heard me at all.

"I don't want to kill anything."

I remembered the crying scene we'd had after he accidentally killed the bug. More watery tears! That was the last thing we needed.

We had to finish this business and find a big box of tissues ASAP.

For some reason, it seemed like everyone had to go talk to the Fathead before we could leave this place. Big Cat still hadn't had his turn, and it now looked as if he had no intention of going in. He scooted to the very back of the room and stood against the wall, shifting from side to side and twirling pieces of his mane around his paw.

I grabbed him by the tail and started pulling him toward the door. He was so scared he actually let me pull him without fighting back.

When we opened the huge door and went into that dark space, I grew scared for a moment, too. Now the Fathead was on fire! Flames blazed from the chair, but the chair itself didn't seem to burn. The heat was so intense we couldn't get very close, although I have to admit we didn't try real hard. I should have felt glad the Fathead was burning up so he couldn't upset Dorothy anymore.

But I wasn't glad. It was just all too strange.

Then a voice roared out of the flames. Big Cat jumped so high the floor shook when he landed. I'm ashamed to say I could feel my tail curl up between my legs. Yeah, I admit it—I was scared. Talking fire is not something you see every day, at least, not in Kansas.

The Fathead wasn't screaming or anything, so I guess he wasn't actually burning up. Had the Fathead turned into a fireball? The voice sounded just the same as before.

"Why are you here?" the Fiery Fathead bellowed.

"I f-forget," Big Cat said, slinking backward toward the door. "I think I'm in the wrong room."

"You came to ask me for something," the Fathead insisted.

"No, no." Big Cat shook his furry head. "I was looking for the bathroom. S-sorry to bother you."

A great booming laugh sounded all around us.

"You want courage," the Fathead said, "but you are too scared to even ask me for it."

Courage? That's what Big Cat was looking for? What an idiot. I mean, yes, he needed it and all, but courage is not something someone can give you. Pork chops, ham bones—those are the kinds of things you could ask for. But courage is the sort of thing you practice and learn, like chasing down a field mouse.

"I can give you courage," the Fiery Fathead promised.

"Don't listen to him!" I barked. "He's a fraud. No one can give you courage. You have to find it for yourself."

But of course, Big Cat couldn't understand me. So, he kept listening to the Fathead.

"You will have to help Dorothy fill the ditch and bring me her something," the Fiery Fathead continued.

"It's only one ditch, right?" I asked, just to clarify. "And we only have to bring one of the whatevers you asked for?" The picture had looked like a stick, but the Fathead used a different word that sounded like pond or frond or something.

Of course, he didn't answer.

"W-what if we can't do it?" Big Cat asked fearfully. "What if we can't fill her?"

The Fiery Fathead fixed him in a withering gaze. "Then you'll be a cow-something forever!"

I guess a cow-something is someone who doesn't have courage. Since he wasn't a cow of any kind now, I didn't think it was likely he'd be one forever, but we were dealing with a flaming head that liked to order people around. So, I couldn't be sure.

Anyway, Big Cat apparently didn't want to hear that he might be a cow-something forever. He turned tail and ran for the door.

"Nice work, Fathead," I called to the fireball in the chair. "He's not going to be able to help much with filling the ditch if he's hiding under a bench somewhere, is he?" Then I hurried after the cat so I wouldn't get left behind.

Back in the shiny part of the palace, someone led us to a room with lots of soft people furniture.

Since no one was paying attention to me, I was able to curl up on a sofa without getting hit with a rolled-up newspaper. And then I guess I fell asleep, because the next thing I knew, I was waking up to the smell of ham and eggs.

Chapter 14

I opened my eyes to see two men come in carrying plates of food that looked as good as it smelled. Besides ham and eggs, there were biscuits—not the hard kind dogs usually get but the soft, warm kind designed for wimpy people-teeth. And strips of crispy bacon. And mounds of fried potatoes.

The men set the plates on a table that was way high off the ground.

All the plates.

They did not set a single one down where I could reach it, even though I barked frantically to point out their mistake.

"If you don't give me some ham now," I threatened one of them, "then I might just have to take a chunk out of your ankle for breakfast."

He finally turned and looked down at me. Then he took a bowl from the table and set it on the floor.

"No," I barked. "I'm feeling fine. No tummy troubles." I did a little dance to demonstrate how well I felt. But he paid no attention and simply turned to head for the door.

He'd given me a bowl of grass.

What did he think I was, a rabbit or something? I only eat grass when I feel the need to add a little fiber to my diet. And this wasn't even fresh grass—it was old and dry, like straw.

"Help, Dorothy!" I barked desperately. "They won't give me any of the food."

Dorothy and the others paid no attention. They went over to the table, still talking about the ditch as if their lives depended on it. As if they were talking about something as important as food. Food that they had, and I didn't.

And the worst of it, of course, is that Metal Man and Strawman didn't even *eat* food. While they talked, what was on their plates just sat there, sending its heavenly aroma down to torture me.

I tried to jump up to the table to suggest that they might consider sharing, but I didn't get much past Dorothy's knee. I couldn't even jump high enough to get to the seat of a chair.

I needed a different plan. If I couldn't go up to the food, I had to make the food come down to me. Or maybe I could just make one of the people come to me.

Trying to ignore the taste, I took a mouthful of the dry grass, trotted over to Strawman and casually dropped the grass by his foot.

"Hey, Itchman," I barked. "Look! Aren't you missing something?" I tugged at his pant leg a little just to make sure I had his attention.

The goal was to make him think I'd pulled out some of his straw so he would reach down to pick it up.

I had to bark and pull for a long time, but finally it worked. He bent all the way down to reach for the "straw," and as soon as he did, I jumped onto his back. Then I ran up toward the table and made a great leap, landing on a platter full of bacon. I managed to eat four pieces before Dorothy hauled me back down to the floor.

"Toto!" She scolded. "You shouldn't something something something." I didn't really pay attention to what she was saying, but then, I didn't really need to. I don't think she was telling me I was a good dog, let's put it that way.

While she was yelling in her angry voice, Metal Man said "Look!" and he pointed to the bowl of grass. Everyone stopped talking.

"Oh, Toto, something something."

I still wasn't paying close enough attention to fully understand, but her tone of voice changed from "bad dog" to "I'm so sorry we left you outside in the cold with the mean cow." She hugged me and gave me an enormous slice of ham.

Life was suddenly very good.

I decided the People Palace, with its soft sofa and big plates of ham was not such a bad place after all.

"You know," I barked after a ham-flavored belch, "if we can't get back to Kansas, maybe it wouldn't be too bad to just stay right here."

But as usual, no one listened to me. As soon as I'd finished my ham, before I even had a chance to beg for eggs or biscuits, everyone got up from the table to leave.

Pretty quickly, I realized we weren't just leaving the breakfast table, we were leaving the People Palace. We walked down a long hallway, then through the entry area where we had waited to see the Fiery Fathead. Everyone looked at the huge dark door as we passed, but no one said anything about it. And then we continued on to the main entrance.

"C'mon, Toto," Dorothy urged as I cast one last longing look behind us toward the rooms with the soft couches and big breakfasts. We were leaving all this comfort—and for what? To go out to a silo in the west to look for a stick in a ditch? Why couldn't we just grab a stick from a nearby ditch and pretend it came

from that place in the west. There are ditches everywhere. I could even dig one so we wouldn't have to go
outside the city at all.

Humans, as I've said many times, are not the
smartest of creatures.

Just before we stepped outside, Dorothy stopped
and handed everyone a pair of glasses from her basket. Well, she didn't hand me mine—she leaned down
and fastened them behind my ears so they pointed
uselessly toward the ground. Fortunately, the light
wasn't as bright as when we'd arrived. The sun constantly darted behind small tufts of clouds as if it
didn't want to be seen. Or maybe it didn't want to see
what was going on below.

That was a creepy thought.

The people of the city were not as reluctant as the
sun. They called and waved as we walked through the
crowded streets. We traveled in the opposite direction
from the way we'd come in originally, so even though
the gate we reached in the wall looked just as much
like a pie as the one we'd come through, I guessed we
were leaving through a different one on the opposite
site of the city. In other words, we'd be going into un-
familiar territory right away.

The pie-gate creaked as it swung outward on its
rusty hinges.

It might be a long time before I ever saw another
pie.

As Dorothy pushed me through the gateway, I
inhaled deeply; but if the gate really was a pie, it was
a nail pie, because all I could smell was weathered
metal.

On the ground, I inhaled the scent of hard clay
and tough grass. Tall shoots of prairie grass clung to
each other in determined clumps between patches of
bare ground. In the distance, dark trees framed a line
of hills stacked up like stairs ahead of us.

We started toward those hills in the west while, throughout the afternoon, the sinking sun made the shadows of the trees stretch forward like long fingers reaching to drag us in. I kind of wished the shadows could push us away instead. It was a really, phenomenally, spectacularly bad idea to go west, away from the soft beds and good food and into who knew what kind of danger. Had they all forgotten the tiger-bears that almost ate us alive? There were probably all kinds of dangerous beasts in the hills ahead. And did we have Unclehenry's shotgun or Auntem's kitchen knives or anything to protect ourselves? No.

We had a girl with virtually useless teeth and claws, a brainless walking bag of tinder, a can on legs who rusts himself if he steps on a bug, and a cat that's even more worthless than most cats.

The only weapon we had was me.

And the sad thing was, they didn't even know it.

As if everything wasn't bad enough, it soon seemed we'd have a nasty storm to contend with. A black cloud rose suddenly in the west, blotting out the fading light of the sun. The cloud moved very rapidly.

And very loudly.

Clouds in Kansas are pretty quiet, except during thunderstorms. But what I could hear now wasn't anything like thunder. It sounded like something I'd never heard before, like air leaking out of tractor tire, but a really big tractor tire. So big the tractor would be impossible to drive.

"Hey, guys," I barked. "Looks like we're in for some serious rain."

Big drops zoomed out of the sky, still making that strange noise. A drop hit me on my behind, and it *hurt*.

It stung, actually.

"Oh, no!" I barked. "The cloud isn't full of rain—it's full of *bees!*"

"Oh, no!" I barked. "The cloud isn't full
of rain—it's full of bees!"

Chapter 15

"Oh! Ouch!" Dorothy jumped around in a circle, waving her basket over her head to scare off the bees.

"Help her, guys," I begged Strawman and Metal Man. I figured bees couldn't do much to them.

But they were sure hurting the rest of us. I swatted with my tail as fast as I could, but there was still one place between my shoulders that I couldn't reach, and the bees kept getting me there.

"Stop!" I barked to the bees as I twisted around to try to keep them off my back. "Why are you doing this to us?"

"MUZZZZZTINGZZZZZ..."

I couldn't really understand what they were saying, and I'm not sure whether they understood me, either. It was hard to focus with the overwhelming drone of bees and the cries of terror from Dorothy.

"Let's cover her up," Strawman suggested to Metal Man. Dorothy crouched down on the ground and Strawman and Metal Man formed a shield over her. I crawled up close to her for protection, too. But whenever the bees tried to sting Metal Man, their stingers got bent, which made them really angry. So, they kept trying to get around him to sting us.

I know Dorothy's afraid of bees, and her sobs nearly made me cry, too. I had to do something.

"Help!" I barked over and over, hoping some of the bees would listen. "Please help us!"

Their buzz only grew more angry and insistent.

But someone else did listen.

"You rfffgln need help?" a voice below me asked.

"Yes," I barked, looking around to see who was talking.

"You rffglb were kind to our cousins, the potato bugs, back fffff in the city. So, if we can rrrrth help you now, we will be glad to return the favor."

The voice came from a bug. It was bigger than the little guys back in the shiny city, but I still didn't see what one lone bug could do against a hoard of killer bees. However, I didn't want to insult him.

"Of course," I barked. "Can you help us get the bees to call off the attack?"

He wriggled violently from side to side. At first I thought he was doing a weird dance or something, but then I realized he was just trying to shake his head. Since it was attached to the rest of his body, he had to shake everything.

"The bees are in a hrrrllff frenzy," he answered. "They won't blifl listen to anyone but their own kind. They're actually rrrbbil like that most of the time, rude little fffffllllns snots."

"So, what can we do?" I asked.

"Eat rrrrllth them," he replied simply.

I gagged. That sounded painful. And even if both of us ate bees for the rest of our lives, we'd never be able to stop them all.

"That's going to take a long time," I said at last.

He shrugged. "Some of my bffllig guys are pretty bbbbliff efficient." He made a whistling sound with his antennae, and suddenly about a million bugs who looked just like him crawled up out of the grass.

"I'm Charlie, rrrfflicc Commander of the A+ Assassin Fffbb Bug Squad, at your service." He turned and started issuing orders to the other bugs in a screechy, high-pitched voice. "Killer, you take your battalion over to the big cat's foot and launch a counter assault. Deadeye, bring your team around to the moving metal pot and fan out from there."

The big bugs spread out, and while the bees were trying to sting us, the assassin bugs began to sort-of sting *them*.

Well, what really happened is that the assassin bugs would suck the insides out of each bee and then move on to another victim. It was a little nauseating, and I kinda wished I had that bowl of grass again. While I was grateful the assassin bugs were helping us, I was also glad they weren't any bigger. And I was *very* glad they considered us friends.

Pretty soon, the bees started to fall back away from us, and before too long, they turned and flew toward the hills in the west.

"Thank you," I barked to as many of the assassin bugs as I could. "You saved us."

"You fllibbss saved one of us, too," Charlie said, licking his lips, or beak, or whatever it was. "So, we're rrflllee even."

"I think we should turn back," I commented as I looked toward the dark hills ahead of us. "This doesn't seem like a very friendly place."

"You're right." Charlie nodded, this time shaking his whole body up and down like he was jumping rope. "it's a rbbllr rotten place. We have never come this far ffflllliw west before, and I doubt we bblblibw will again." He looked around for a moment, as if he expected to see another cloud of bees on the horizon. Finally, he turned back to face me. "The creatures rbbrrih here do not think for themselves," he said. "Someone is bbffllllicc controlling them."

"Who?" I barked.

He straightened his wings, looking as if he were getting ready to take off.

"I don't fllibbbw want to stay long enough to find out."

"Could it be a thing with the ugly face? Are we close to a big silo with water around it?"

"Haven't seen it," Charlie answered as he kicked off from the ground. "But I haven't rbbllb been in the direction you're going. Good-ffllibb bye," he called. "And rrrbbbg good luck."

I had a feeling we were going to need it.

Chapter 16

No one really felt like going anywhere after the fierce bee attack.

I take that back—none of us felt like going *forward*. I definitely wanted to go *back* to the People Palace with the ham and eggs.

But the others refused to follow me when I started back toward the city. So, we just walked a little bit more, to the first line of trees nestled against the hills. We huddled together to sleep at the base of a big tree that night.

When we woke in the morning, I was hungry, but I didn't feel like eating. The words of the assassin bugs had echoed in my dreams all night. The creatures all around were under the control of something.

That couldn't be good.

We started to move westward again, but when we came to the crest of the first hill, I saw a sight that crashed my hopes more thoroughly than a blind pig driving a tractor. There, silhouetted against a dark sky, was an even darker tall silo in the midst of smaller ones surrounded by a forbidding high wall. From this distance, it looked like thorny branches jutting out from an enormous sticker bush. If it had been a plant, it would probably be the type that made you itch or sting if you touched it.

But I didn't think the black thing was a plant. I was pretty sure it was what we'd seen a picture of back in the room with the Fathead, and I didn't think it was anything like the silo on our farm.

With each step we took, the thorns looked bigger and uglier.

This was not a good idea, and I said so, even though I knew no one could understand me.

"We shouldn't go this way," I barked.

Dorothy shook her head. "No, I'm saving the rest of the bacon for tomorrow."

"There won't *be* a tomorrow for us if we keep going in this direction," I pointed out.

Metal Man patted me on the head. "I think Toto's cold. He's shivering."

I gave him this look.

"I'm shivering because I'm scared, you silly tub of tin. Only a fool wouldn't be scared after what we've been through. We should go *that* way." I pointed my nose toward the friendlier-looking grasslands in the north. "I'll bet the people there don't live in buildings shaped like sticker bushes."

But Dorothy just bent down, scooped me into her arms and carried me forward. Toward the dark hills and the thorny building in the west.

We walked for hours. Or maybe it just seemed like hours because I was so unhappy. There were no bacon or pork chops in our future, I could just tell. In fact, as I said earlier, I seriously doubted there would *be* much of a future.

Nothing seemed to live in this land. I heard no bugs or birds or chickens or anything. I smelled no animal poop of any kind, and that was really weird.

This eerie silence continued all morning. Then, at midday, I heard the faint sound of feet. Lots of feet, like a cattle stampede, headed straight toward us from the west. But the scent that came toward us on the wind had nothing to do with beef. It smelled more like other dogs. Angry dogs.

"I don't like this, Dorothy," I growled. "We need to turn around before those dogs get too close."

As the smell grew nearly overpowering, I suddenly realized they were *mad* dogs. We had no choice now. We had to get away, or we would be torn to shreds.

"Let's get out of here!" I barked frantically.

But they all kept walking, right toward the beasts.

"Are you crazy?"

Still they wouldn't listen. But I couldn't wait any longer. I turned and ran.

I had tried to warn the others we should go back, but they wouldn't listen. Now it was time to save myself.

"Toto, stop!" Dorothy screamed. "Come back!"

But I kept going. Distant howls came from behind me as I ran. The sound of pounding feet grew louder way too fast. The mad dogs must be big, with much longer legs than mine, so they could run much faster. They would catch up with the others—and even me—very soon.

An overpowering aroma of bad breath swept over me as the mad dogs drew closer. It was the stench from mouths that had eaten something rotten and wanted something fresh. My heart pounded so fiercely I could barely breathe, but I kept running. I had to get away. I had to!

And Dorothy? She only had two legs. She couldn't run as fast. The mad dogs would catch her for certain. Some of them would chase Big Cat, and some would dull their teeth on Metal Man, but then they'd all turn on poor Dorothy. They'd even rip Strawman to pieces like a tissue from a trashcan. All of them would be helpless against the wild mad dogs.

Those poor fools didn't even know how to talk to dogs. If they begged for mercy or tried to bargain with key information about the location of pork chops, the dogs would hear nothing but "something something chop."

They could do nothing to save themselves.

But *I* could.

I could talk to the mad dogs.

My run slowed to a trot as I turned to look behind me. The others were running now, running away from a huge pack of crazed dogs that looked so wild they might have been wolves. The pack covered the hillside. There were so many gray beasts the woods seemed alive with snarling fur.

And only *I* could talk to them. Or try to. They might eat me for lunch if they didn't feel like listening.

All at once, I knew I had to try. I was the only one of the group who had any chance of calling off the attack. And from the smell, I knew the wild dogs meant to attack.

So, I turned all the way around and ran toward the snarling masses. I looked for their leader, the one the others would follow. If I could convince him to stop, the others would.

Hopefully.

"What's going on?" I barked as I headed toward them, staggering a little as my paws got tangled in the dense underbrush. "What are you guys doing?"

"Did you hear something, Happy?" The lead dog turned to the companion on his left.

"Yeah, dude. It came from over there," an extra-scruffy-looking dog answered. Apparently, that was Happy.

The lead dog sniffed the air, pointing his nose high.

"I smell a dog," he said.

I started jumping up and down so he would be able to *see* a dog, too.

"Hey, look at that little guy!" A female smiled as she looked at me. "He's so cute."

Well, I guess I wasn't going to scare these big guys, so I'd have to accept "cute" and work with it. I added a little twist to my jump.

"What are you doing here?" the female dog called sternly. "You could get hurt."

They were still far enough away I figured they might only be able to hear me while I was jumping up above the underbrush.

"Don't..." I said as I jumped, "...eat..." I could only manage one word on each jump. "...my...friends!" I begged. Having made an enormous jump with each word, I was pretty worn out by the time I finished.

"What did he say?" the lead dog asked.

"Don't eat his French toast?" the female suggested.

"No, man," Happy corrected her, "he said, like, don't *heat* his French toast."

"What's French toast?" the lead dog asked.

The female shrugged. "Ask him."

"Call off (pant-pant) the attack!" I begged as I ran up to them. "Tell your dogs not to attack my friends."

"Dogs!" the leader huffed indignantly. "We are the Witch's Wolves."

Well, that explained why they looked as wild as wolves and why they smelled a little mad. As the assassin bug had told me, they were under the control of something. The witch.

"What's a witch?" I asked.

"She is the ruler of this land," the lead dog said with obvious pride.

"So, she's like a mayor?" This might not be so bad. Women could often be charmed by the wag of a dog's tail.

The female dog shook her head. "She has more power than that. She uses magic to control her realm."

"Magic?" I wasn't sure I understood. "Like pulling a rabbit out of a hat and finding coins in people's ears?" I'd seen a magic show at the state fair but I couldn't see how you could control anyone with migrating coins and a few rabbits.

"No, dude," Happy corrected. "Like turning a rabbit *into* a hat and making people's ears explode. She's wicked."

"Oh." This magic sounded a little more menacing than anything I'd seen back in Kansas. "Does she live in a dark silo surrounded by water?"

The leader looked confused, like he didn't know what a silo was.

"Well," Happy said, "like, the water's not right next to the main castle tower, but..."

So, we weren't going all this way to a stone silo to get a stick from a ditch. We were going to a castle to take a stick from a witch. And if she could control creatures, she could throw that stick and keep making us bring it back over and over until we died from boredom.

Things were making a lot more sense now, but I think I actually liked it better when they didn't.

The Witch controlled the bees, so she'd probably sent them to attack us. And when that didn't work, she sent her wolves.

They would probably have eaten me already if they hadn't thought I was so cute.

"I'm sorry," I said, hoping I hadn't insulted them too badly by calling them dogs. "I've never smelled a wolf before. Now I understand why you have such a powerful aroma." Horrible, too, of course, but I didn't have to mention that. "Can you forgive my mistake?"

"Yes." The lead wolf nodded graciously.

"Oh, good." I sighed with relief. "So, you won't attack my friends?"

The lead wolf sniffed derisively. "Of course, we'll still attack your friends. The Witch ordered us to kill all of you."

"And she's, you know, the Witch, so we, like, have to listen to her, you know?" Happy added.

"*Why* do you have to listen to her?" I asked, looking at each of them in turn. "Do you *want* to kill all of us?"

Happy shook his head. "Like, no, man," he said sadly.

"Well, not you, at least," the female added. "You're cute."

"They're *all* cute, once you get to know them," I insisted. And I was startled to realize I meant it. Was I starting to kind-of like them? Okay, maybe *like* was too strong. I felt sorry for them.

"We have to kill *someone*," the leader pointed out.

"But not the pretty one," the female nodded toward Dorothy. "The Witch wants us to bring her back alive."

"Whoa." Happy turned to look at her. "It's, like, a good thing you remembered that before we ate her or something."

"The Witch wants Dorothy as a prisoner?" I barked.

"Yeah," Happy nodded. "I think she wants to know where she got her shiny shoes. She wants a pair."

"How about if she just takes off the shoes and you take them back to the Witch?" I suggested.

"No," the leader insisted, "I think if that would have worked she would have told us just to bring the shoes. But she wanted the whole girl, alive. So, we must obey."

"Can you just pretend you killed the others?" I pleaded.

Happy shook his head. "No way, dude. The Witch can, like, see everything with her magic crystal round thing. She'd know if we disobeyed her."

"How about if we stage a pretend battle," I suggested, "and we pretend to die and you pretend to take Dorothy back and she runs away?"

He shrugged. "That'd work, I guess."

"Except," the female pointed out, "that the Witch can *hear* everything we say, too, so she knows you suggested this."

Happy sank down onto his haunches. "Oh, rats!"

"She's not going to be real thrilled that we're standing around talking instead of eating you right now," the female added.

"You know," I said quickly, "we won't taste very good. Especially the guy made of metal. He's like a can of food with no food inside."

"Bummer," Happy said sadly.

I stepped closer to him and lowered my voice. "But I do know where you can find lots of good food. Ham and pork chops every day."

His ears perked up. "Seriously?"

"Oh, yeah." I nodded. "All you have to do is head east, to a city with great shiny buildings. Then you have to settle down and pretend to be pet dogs."

"I get it." He turned to the others. "Then when they let us in, we attack and take all the food."

"Well, you could do that," I admitted, "but I think you'd do better if you kept on pretending to be pets. As long as they think you're pets, they'll keep bringing you more food. If you kill the people, then you're on your own. No one to get food for you."

He considered that for a moment. "Good point."

"So, what do you think?" I asked hopefully.

He shrugged again. "Sure." Again he turned to the others. "I mean, the food's gotta be better than what we get at Witchified Castle."

After a moment, the other wolves began to nod in agreement, and I heard someone talking about pork chops.

"Thanks for not attacking us," I called to the pack as the lead wolf turned them all east toward the shiny city.

The female came over and nudged me on the top of the head.

"Hey, Cutie, thanks for the tip about the food," she said.

"Later, dude," Happy called as he started off.

I sighed with relief as I watched them go. While it was a little insulting being called "Cutie," it sure was better than being eaten.

We were safe.

Until the Witch sent something else after us.

Chapter 17

After being attacked by bees and wolves, you'd think Dorothy and her friends would take the hint and turn around. The Witch was trying to kill us—her own wolves had told us so. Plus, she was a witch, with fierce powers, mighty armies, a castle fortress and probably really bad breath.

We, on the other hand, had no powers, no army, and a small wooden house that had suffered considerable wind damage and that, anyway, we'd left behind somewhere near a cornfield.

Our breath might have been as bad as hers.

Even so, we were still no match for her. We needed to keep as far away from this witch as possible.

Instead, we were going right to her castle. Hiking through forest so thick with branches and vines Metal Man had to chop a path with his axe. The woods smelled like rot, like rats that had been dead so long they didn't even smell interesting anymore. Just... dead. It was the smell of death, I decided. Still, if we could smell it, at least that meant we weren't dead yet ourselves.

That cheered me up a little.

Then Dorothy offered me a piece of leftover bacon, and the world suddenly seemed much brighter. Maybe the creatures around here weren't in the control of a wicked witch but just a semi-wicked witch. Or maybe a not-very-wicked whippet. Or maybe even a not-at-all-wicked walrus.

I liked that idea a lot. I would have no trouble outrunning a walrus.

But my optimism didn't last much longer than the bacon.

With every step, I listened for the sound of a new attack. What would it be this time? Killer birds zooming in from the grey skies? Venomous snakes slithering up from the forest floor? A brigade of firemen shooting giant water cannons full of bubble bath? My guts twisted as I thought of new possibilities.

When would it come? The waiting was almost worse than any attack could be. I savored each breath as if it were my last. Though I wanted to walk slowly, I kept up with Dorothy's brisk pace, enjoying her closeness for however much longer it would last. She smelled like fresh hay and sunshine and a clean bowl full of dog food. And snuggles on a cold windy night. She was everything in the world to me, and I was determined now to stay with her no matter what happened. Even if I had the chance to escape, I wouldn't. I would stay with her until the end.

And then I heard it coming.

Not the buzz of bees or the snarls of wolves, but the chatter of...I didn't know what. Chattering things. The noise rapidly grew louder as the things approached from the west. It sounded like it might be chipmunks, or parakeets or even monkeys. I couldn't see anything through the dense canopy of trees overhead. It was all just noise. Though I watched closely for any sign of movement, I saw no creatures yet. But

I could hear them, their racket growing louder with each passing second.

"*Eeeeaahhhheeeaaah!*"

They were apparently going to annoy us to death.

That doesn't sound too bad, probably, unless you've been there. We were drowned in the sound of mindless chatter, of noise that should add up to something that makes sense but doesn't. Pain started in my ears and stabbed through my head until I thought I would explode.

As the noise got close, I could tell it was coming from above, but it didn't sound like birds. Was it bats? Monkeys swinging through the trees? I still could see nothing overhead.

Then, they started swooping down. It *was* monkeys. Big monkeys. They looked like creepy plastic toys, and not just because of their weird nasty grins. Because they also had wings. Great huge wings coming right out of the middle of their backs. They were *flying* monkeys.

For a moment, what I saw convinced me the whole thing had to be a dream. Big cowardly cats I could believe. Even talking men made of metal and straw. Yeah, they didn't have 'em in Kansas, but we weren't in Kansas anymore. But flying monkeys? No way.

I had to admit, though, those monkeys really could fly. Two of them lifted Metal Man as if he weighed no more than an empty soda can. "*Eeeaahhheeeaahh!*" With a great chattering cry, they carried him high into the hills and disappeared.

Now, there were four of us, and this place seemed even weirder than before.

More monkeys landed. As I stayed close to protect Dorothy, two of them grabbed Strawman and started pulling him apart.

"No!" Dorothy screamed. "Oh, no!"

"Stop!" I barked. "You can't just tear someone to pieces like that."

But they kept right on. They split him into sections, separating his legs from his chest and pulling out his straw stuffing as if they planned to build a nest from his insides. It was sickening. After a while, I couldn't watch anymore.

Only three of us now.

It took four monkeys to pick up Big Cat.

"Not gonna get me, you something something something monkeys," he roared. He scratched and snarled and fought harder than I expected. Even when they came after him with tomahawks, he kept fighting, so maybe he wasn't as much of a scaredy-cat as I'd thought.

Finally, three monkeys grabbed him and held him by the tail, his mane and his back so he couldn't bite or scratch them. Then they carried *him* away to the west.

Two of us.

The flying monkeys had breath even worse than the wolves. I learned that when one of them picked me up by the nape of the neck and held me up to look at me. I snarled in his face and am embarrassed to say this only seemed to make his grin get wider, as if he were about to laugh at me. As he tucked me under his arm and crouched to take off, I looked around for Dorothy, but she was already gone.

I hoped we were going to the same place.

Chapter 18

The monkey carried me in his arms the way Dorothy does, but I didn't feel safe and comfortable like when she carries me. I felt sad.

Miserable.

Depressed.

And it only got worse the longer we flew.

As we were soaring over a gorge that looked as deep as the one we had crossed on the tree trunk when the black tiger-bear things were chasing us, I heard the clatter of metal on rocks. I looked down to see that the monkeys who had been carrying Metal Man had dropped him, and he smashed against the rocks as he fell deeper and deeper. After a few seconds, I couldn't see him anymore, but I could hear his hollow clang for a long time. I felt sick inside. Even if he wasn't smashed to pieces, he would never be able to get out.

I was shocked at the monkeys' cruelty and even more shocked to find how bad I felt when I realized I would never see Metal Man again. I'd thought I hadn't even really liked him, but now I knew that I did. At least, sort of. He'd stopped calling me "little," and he was always very careful not to step on my tail.

And now he was gone forever.

It was cold up there in the sky, but I don't think that's really why I started shivering. We had seen Strawman torn to shreds, and now Metal Man lay battered and trapped in a deep chasm. Big Cat was nowhere in sight. What was going to happen to us?

At least I knew Dorothy would be safe for a little while—that is, until the Witch got her shoes.

I figured the monkeys would take Dorothy directly to the Witch's tower, and me, too, probably. Had they taken Big Cat there? Would they kill him and use him for food? What did monkeys eat, anyway? I thought they only liked bananas; but then, I'd also thought they couldn't fly, and I was certainly wrong about that.

They might have dropped the cat down into the big ditch, just like Metal Man. He wouldn't make much noise, so we might never know it had happened. But I bet he would snarl and fight, and we would probably have heard that. So, I grew hopeful he hadn't been dropped.

Yet.

Eventually, we flew up so high we could almost touch the grey clouds that rolled together like bubbles boiling in a pot. Cracks of lightning zipped across overhead. These monkeys were crazy—flying in a storm. We might get electrocuted. Or hit by a house or something.

I hoped the flashes of lightning hadn't hit Metal Man, because that would have really hurt.

Down below us, the hills grew darker and steeper. A river of black rushing water cut through the ground as we drew closer to the thorny black buildings that must be the Witch's castle. I could see that the river had been channeled to surround the castle like a moving moat.

The aroma of frog water gradually became stronger, along with a salty smell like blood from a fresh cut. I didn't like that moat at all. It made me wonder what would happen to us after the Witch took Dorothy's shoes. Would the monkey drop me into the moat? I think I would have rather faced the bottomless rocky gorge. Nothing could be worse than the rushing water that surrounded the castle.

Before I knew it, we were there. We soared over the outer walls and above empty courtyards covered with gravel. The buildings that had looked like black thorns from a distance were really a deep gray, like the sky during the worst thunderstorms. In one of the courtyards, I saw a row of cages like the ones they use for the big animals at the State Fair. But the cages all looked empty, and there was no happy sense of anticipation or cotton candy like at the fair.

Just before we turned away from there, I thought I might have seen a large animal in the last cage, but it was hard to tell because, at that moment, we flew toward the tallest tower in the very center of the castle. Ahead, the monkeys carried Dorothy toward an open window. The towers were made of flat stone that seemed to suck the light and heat out of the air and swallow it into nothingness. I hoped we wouldn't be swallowed into nothingness, too. Because now the monkey was carrying *me* inside the same window where Dorothy had just disappeared.

The smell of frog water and dried blood nearly took my breath away as we landed inside the tower. Dusty shelves lined the room all around, and those shelves were packed with bottles of things I didn't want to look at too closely. One seemed to be full of pickled mice.

On a table lay the headless body of a cat, and as much as I dislike cats, I still hated to think of how that one might have ended its life, being terrorized by this stinky witch. I think there was a short gnarled stick on the table, too. It might have been the one the Fathead had showed us. But I only got a glance at it as we flew into the room.

The Witch's foul smell was noticeable right away, but I couldn't really see what she looked like other than that she was tall and covered with raggedy clothes. She wore a dark shapeless dress that hung nearly to the floor, and her head was covered with a scraggley old shawl, like a poor woman going to church. When she turned to face us, the first thing I noticed were her bony hands reaching out from the sleeves of her dress. I shrank back against the monkey who was carrying me, because I thought she was reaching out to take me out of his arms. But soon I realized she was reaching for Dorothy.

"Don't even think of touching my girl, you hag!" I barked. "Or I'll bite your nose off and suck out your eyeballs." Yeah, my threat was a little more graphic than usual—I think the sight of all the creepy body parts in the jars all around the room was starting to get to me.

Anyway, after that, the monkey set me down, so I wasn't going to be biting anything other than ankles.

Even from down on the ground, though, I could tell that the Witch's face looked just like the picture the Fathead had shown us. Had he known she would come after us, and that she'd destroy Strawman and Metal Man? Had he known how cruel and dangerous she was? I think he did. And still he sent a *girl*, a young girl with no real teeth or claws, to face her.

From that moment on, I hated the Fathead almost as much as I hated the Witch.

Stretching her long bony fingers to their fullest length, the Witch pointed at Dorothy's shoes.

"Those shoes should be mine."

Well, she didn't waste any time, did she? Of course, the wolves had told us the Witch wanted Dorothy for her shoes.

I hoped she wouldn't give them to her.

And she didn't, at least not right away.

The Witch pointed again.

"Give me those shoes!" she growled.

Dorothy shook her head no, but she was trembling with fright and probably too scared to be able to even talk back to the witch.

The Witch picked the gnarled stick up off the table and pointed it at the shoes a third time. Now I knew what was going to happen. She was going to throw that stick and make Dorothy go pick it up. And then, when she brought it back, the witch would throw it away again. It was a cruel game, but if I could handle it, I figured Dorothy could, too, as long as it didn't go on too long.

But the Witch didn't throw the stick. She just sort of shook it. Maybe she didn't know how to throw properly.

I sure wasn't about to teach her.

After a while, she seemed to grow very angry at the stick. She shouted out some words I think I once heard Unclehenry use when the tractor wouldn't start. Then she banged the stick against the table. That made the dead cat's head roll off the edge, and it bounced a couple of times on the dirty stone floor before rolling under a shelf.

With a shriek of frustration, the Witch banged the stick on the table again, and then leaned down and smacked it against Dorothy's left shoe. A miniature bolt of lightning shot out from the end of the stick. So, the stick was magic! Or were the shoes magic? The shoes were important, obviously, but I think if they'd been magical, the Fathead back in the Shiny City would have kept them for himself instead of sending Dorothy to collect the Witch's stick.

Maybe the stick and the shoes were only magical when they were used together. So, if the Witch had both, she might become tremendously powerful.

Fortunately for us, the magic stick didn't seem to be working at the moment. The bolt of lightning had come out of the end that was in the Witch's hand, so she howled in pain and grabbed it as if it was burned. The stick fell to the floor and rolled under the shelf with the cat head.

I'm not sure why the Witch just didn't grab hold of Dorothy and yank the shoes off her feet if she wanted them so badly. Maybe the magic in them somehow protected Dorothy. Instead of trying to force the shoes from her, the Witch just stamped her own foot in frustration and stared longingly at those shiny shoes.

Her stare was odd—one eye focused on the target, but the other wandered around as if it were seeing other things or nothing at all. I couldn't look at her face for very long without feeling kind of sick.

I figured then maybe she'd have her monkeys try to take the shoes away from Dorothy. But when I looked around, I discovered many of them were gone, and the others were flexing their wings in preparation for take-off. The last monkey to leave pointed at something on one of the shelves, and then leaned forward to laugh in the Witch's face.

Wow. I didn't expect that. I thought she controlled them, like she seemed to control everything else. Even if she couldn't control them, I thought it was pretty stupid to risk making her mad, though. But I guess, since they had wings and she didn't, they weren't worried about her catching them any more than the crows were worried about me catching them back home.

Back home seemed impossibly far away now.

I tried not to think about it. Instead, since no one was paying any attention to me, I scooted over near the shelf where the monkey had pointed, trying very hard not to picture what had rolled underneath it.

If I leaned back and stretched up on the tips of my paws, I could see that, on top of the shelf next to bottles of dried beetles, there was something that looked like an old hat. It was squashed a bit, like Unclehenry's hat after it blew from his head just as Auntem was getting into the farm wagon to go to church one summer morning. Auntem sat on it and crushed it flat. For the rest of the day, every time Dorothy looked at him, she started to laugh.

I wondered if she would ever laugh like that again.

Oh, no. I was still thinking about home even though I tried not to.

Instead, I made myself look around the cold, creepy room. The Witch was now reading something in a crumbling old book. She mumbled to herself, frowning, and she was getting more and more angry.

Although Dorothy had crossed her arms and tried to appear brave when the Witch demanded her shoes, now she was biting her lip and trying not to look scared to pieces. I could smell her fear clearly, despite the stinkiness of all the weird witchy things in the room. She was terrified.

When the Witch finished reading whatever was in her book, she slammed it shut. Pursing her lips, she took a deep breath and gave a loud whistling noise that made my hair stand on end. Then she took off her shoes. She wasn't wearing striped socks like the other witch; in fact, she had no socks on at all. Just gray bony feet with long cracked toenails. She eyed Dorothy's shiny shoes as if they were a pork chop on the kitchen table.

Chapter 19

But the magic stick had rolled under the same shelf as the you-know-what. Did I really want to reach under there?

Stupid question. But I had to.

Bracing myself, in case I encountered any cat eyeballs or fur stiffened with dried blood, I leaned down and stuck my paw under the shelf to see if I could reach the stick. There were some sticky things there, and something really slimy, but I tried not to think about what they might be and just kept feeling around until I had the Witch's stick. I rolled it out and looked at it.

It was brown and bent and almost as long as me. But it didn't weigh much at all, and instead of wood, it smelled like dried blood.

The Witch made that awful whistling noise again, and soon the door opened and in walked the strangest creature I'd ever seen in my life. Its hands were human, but once the door was open, the creature dropped down on all fours to walk. It had a long lean body like a cheetah, but with stripes like a tiger and a lion's mane. However, its head was like a penguin's, so that it didn't look much like a big cat at all. Its neck was unusually long, not as much as a giraffe but enough to make the creature appear unbalanced. It was so odd-looking that, for a moment, I wasn't even afraid of it.

"Take her goo blah kitchen," the Witch ordered pointing toward the door.

The creature nodded and looked Dorothy over with a sneer. Then it inclined its penguin head toward the door as if to indicate that Dorothy should follow as it turned and went back out.

Dorothy understood, and hurried after it. She didn't look around for me, but I assumed that was because she was so scared. Anyway, I picked up the stick and ran over to join her, and she looked grateful to have me with her.

She stuffed the Witch's stick into her basket, and then we followed the strange striped creature down a long spiral staircase until we reached the bottom. We crossed a floor of moldy marble tiles and came to a door leading into a big dark room that smelled like smoke and rotten vegetables. The Witch's kitchen.

The creature pointed to a stack of dirty dishes, and I guess Dorothy decided it meant for her to wash them. She pumped water into the sink, picked up a metal plate coated with dried crusty stuff and started to scrub with her fingernails, since there was no dishcloth.

"No, *ah-caw!*" the creature squawked in a deep voice that sounded like a rooster inside a cave. "Wash it! Wash it!"

I was relieved to realize I could understand him.

Dorothy didn't seem to be able to, though. She jumped back in terror and shook her head.

"I don't something something."

"You need to wash those dishes," the creature ordered. He grabbed a wooden bowl, held it up to his beak and started to lick it.

For a moment, I was fascinated. I didn't know penguins had such long tongues.

"See? Wash," the creature explained. "Just like this."

"She *was* trying to wash it," I informed him. "Humans don't know how to use their tongues very well. So, they have to use their hands instead."

The creature turned to me. "*A-caw!* She's a human, you say? Is she your slave?"

"She's more of a pet, really."

He nodded in understanding. "Inferior creatures like her don't make good slaves. They don't understand what you need them to do." He waved toward the water and rubbed the bowl to demonstrate she could wash it that way if she had to.

I sighed with relief. It sure was nice to meet someone who could sympathize with me.

"I think if I could teach Dorothy to talk or at least understand speech," I explained, "I could probably get more out of her."

The creature sat back on his hind legs so he was upright. "Yes, it is a shame she only knows the witch-talk."

"What's the witch-talk?" I asked.

He watch Dorothy scratch at crusted residue on a plate.

"The sounds she makes when she talks to her prisoners."

"Can she talk to you?" I asked him. "I mean, *really* talk?"

The creature shook his furry mane disdainfully. "She *a-caw* cannot make the sounds, since her mouth is shaped like the mouth of your poor human. But she can say things directly into our minds, and make us do things whether we want to or not."

I remembered what the wolves said about the Witch controlling them. I assumed she had controlled the bees, and somehow controlled the monkeys. But they had left. So, maybe she could only control them for a short time.

I couldn't imagine how it would feel to have the Witch practically living inside your head.

"That sounds awful," I said.

His big eyes stared straight at me. "You have no idea."

I cringed at the pain behind his words. But then I thought about the monkeys again.

"Did the Witch control the flying monkeys, too?" I asked. "How could they just leave?"

"She *a-caw* could call on them three times to ask them to complete tasks for her," the creature explained as he pulled a pair of grasshopper legs out of his mane. "Bringing you in was the third task."

"Three times?" I asked. "That's pretty random."

He shrugged. "It was a magic hat, I think. She put it on each time before she called them."

That's why the monkeys had looked at it as they left. The Unclehenry hat.

Right now, I would have loved to hear Unclehenry roar at me in the growling angry voice he used whenever I scared the chickens or chewed too much on someone's shoes. He was so far away now! I felt very lonely, even though my girl was just a few feet away. This dark, dank place seemed to suck all the hope right out of me. I guess, if you're keeping prisoners, though, you want them to feel that way.

Were we the only ones being kept in this depressing place?

"Are there other prisoners here now?" I asked.

"Only one," the creature answered. "A great big furry *a-caw* cat."

"So, he *is* here!"

The creature nodded its smooth feathered head.

"I thought he was with you, since the monkeys brought him in about the same time. But he snarls and snaps at us whenever we try to talk to him. So, I don't think he's civilized."

I nodded in agreement. "He *is* with us, and he's *not* very civilized. He's like the humans, doesn't know how to talk properly."

But although he was a cat, and an inferior non-speaking one at that, I was still really glad he was here and that he was safe. Or at least as safe as any of us.

All at once, the creature, who had been sitting up and speaking in such a dignified way, dropped down on all fours, ran over to the corner and darted his head forward to snatch a large dragonfly off the wall. His long neck gave him quite a reach, and his sharp beak snapped the big bug in two just like a pair of scissors.

He came back over and offered me half of the insect. I politely declined.

"So, um, if you don't mind my asking, what sort of creature are you?" I was a little nervous, since he might be insulted that I didn't immediately recognize his kind. "We don't have anything as, um, magnificent as you back home. I assume you know that I'm a dog."

"I am a lickloe," he said, dragonfly wings drooping out of either side of his beak. He swallowed the insect in a great gulp. "And you may *a-caw* call me Lomen. Where is home?"

"Kansas."

He let out a belch. "That's on the other side of Oz, isn't it?"

"*Way* on the other side," I agreed. So, that bug really had told me the name of the place. We were in Oz. I didn't know where Oz was, but I figured that compared to here, Kansas was way on the other side of everything.

"So, how'd you end up in this part of Oz?" the lickloe asked. "I mean, I know the monkeys brought you to the castle, but how did you get close enough for the Witch to see you? Her good eye can only see about ten miles."

"She can see things ten miles away?" I asked in surprise.

He nodded. "When she's paying attention."

Yikes! It was like the Witch had super-eyes or something.

"Can she see things up close real well with the other eye?" I asked, growing more worried by the second.

"As far as I can tell," the lickloe drawled, "she can't see at all with the other eye."

"So," I said with relief, "you could peck out her good eye and then she'd be blind."

"In theory, yes." He didn't seem too enthused by the idea. "She wouldn't let me, though. Since she controls me."

"Oh." I'd forgotten that part. "Does she know what you're saying to me now?"

"If she's paying attention."

I sighed. "Rats."

"Where?" He sat up and licked his beak. "I haven't had a rat in ages."

"Not a real rat," I explained. "It's just a thing we say back in Kansas. When we're frustrated."

I would have to watch everything I said to the lickloes, since the Witch could read their minds. It meant that, if I were going to plan anything, I would have to work with Dorothy or Big Cat. And neither of them could understand any plan I tried to explain to them.

This wasn't going to be easy.

In walked the strangest creature I'd ever
seen in my life

Chapter 20

Since the Witch could read Lomen's mind, I couldn't tell him we had come to her castle to kill her and steal her stick. So, I was glad he didn't ask again.

Instead, he offered to take me on a tour. While Dorothy washed dishes, he showed me around the worker's quarters on the second floor. There was no furniture in their rooms, only flattened piles of straw.

The lickloes who worked as night guards lay curled up on their straw beds, and at first I thought they were asleep. But then I noticed that one of them was slowly rolling a small red berry back and forth on the floor with his tail. He was humming a sad tune— humming really wasn't the right word for it, though. The sound was immensely sad, like the keening of a puppy who knows he will never see his mother again.

"Is he okay?" I asked Lomen softly.

The lickloe shrugged. "He is himself."

"But he seems upset about something. Really depressed."

Lomen fixed me in that intense bird-like stare of his. "He is a lickloe. It would be wrong for him to be happy."

"Oh. Okay. I didn't know about the not-supposed-to-be happy thing. As I said before, we don't have any lickloes back home."

"Of course not. There are no lickloes anyplace but here."

"The Witch has all the lickloes? In the whole world?" No wonder they were depressed.

Lomen nodded. "We used to live in the meadow on the north side of the forest. Then she came. At first she took just the hills. Then the woods. And then she came for us."

"She took all of you? The whole village, er, tribe, er pack, or clan, or whatever of you?"

He sighed and looked out the window for a moment.

"She put out poisoned grasshoppers for us—one of our favorite fun foods. We all ate and ate and had a great time and no one stopped to think about why there were so many grasshoppers out all at once." He turned back to face me. "The poison put us to sleep, and when we woke up, we were here, inside the castle."

"All of you?"

He nodded. "When we found out we couldn't escape, most of our pack jumped off the castle wall and drowned themselves in the moat. What you see here is all that is left of us."

I had counted about twenty beds in the two rooms. There were only twenty lickloes left in the whole world, and the Witch had them all under her control.

I shivered as I glanced toward the window and thought about the dark rushing water of the moat outside. No wonder the lickloe had hummed such a sad song.

Only twenty of their kind left, and all slaves to the Witch.

I grew a little hopeful when I realized those were about the only creatures she seemed to have in her control any more. The wolves had all gone to the Shiny City, and the monkeys had flown away. And I guess the bees were all dead.

It seemed to me the Witch was sort of helpless if all she could control all the time were those twenty lickloes.

Of course, that was twenty more lickloes than I could control. All I had was an overgrown cat who was locked up and a girl who couldn't talk right and had to wash dishes with her hands.

She was still working when we got back to the kitchen. When she finished, she sat down in the corner to rest. There were no chairs in the room. I guess lickloes don't need them since they just sit back on their hind legs.

"So, those were probably the dinner dishes, huh?" I asked Lomen. "We've had kind of a busy day and lost track of time." I hoped he'd take the hint and offer us some leftover dinner.

"Yeah." Lomen sniffed. "Well, since she worked, I guess I *a-caw* can give you something to eat now. Prisoners are allowed to eat after they work."

"Will Dorothy be locked up in a cage like Big Cat?" I asked anxiously. I suppose I should have worried I might be locked up, too, but I figured I could probably squeeze between the bars. The diet of stale bread and grass was making me even scrawnier than I'd been back in Kansas. I was glad the farmyard animals couldn't see me now—I'd be hearing runt jokes for the rest of my life.

The lickloe considered for a moment.

"I don't know if your human will be put in a *a-caw* cage. She doesn't look too dangerous. And the Witch wants those nice shoes she's wearing. The cages aren't the cleanest places, if you know what I mean. So, she might let the girl stay inside with us."

"That would be good." I sighed with relief. Big Cat had fur to keep him warm on a windy cold night, but poor Dorothy was nearly bald. "Hey," I pointed out, "you let the fire go out. Does that mean you don't need to heat hot water for baths?"

"What's a bath?" Lomen asked, stretching his long legs forward and inspecting his fingernails for dirt.

"Really?" Did I believe my ears? "You don't have baths here?" Maybe the Witch's castle wouldn't turn out to be so bad after all.

"I wouldn't know, would I?" Lomen sniffed derisively. "If you won't tell me what they are."

"A bath," I explained "is where you take a tub full of water and get all wet and washed up."

"Ah." Lomen nodded. "Just the way the human washed the dishes. We lickloes wash ourselves properly, just like we do dishes."

I understood what he meant. A tongue bath. The only real way to clean.

"And the Witch doesn't wash at all," Lomen continued. "Doesn't have the tongue for it, I guess."

"She doesn't wash in a tub like humans?"

"Does she *smell* like she ever washes?" Lomen asked.

"No," I admitted.

"And if she did, I would know because we lickloes would have to *a-caw* carry the water for her. We don't even have a tub."

Hurray! No danger of a bath while we were here.

"We just have that bucket, there, for washing the floors." He nodded toward a battered wooden bucket in the corner.

All at once the lickloe's expression became very serious. He leapt over to the corner and pulled Dorothy to her feet.

"She's coming," he hissed.

Frightened, Dorothy jerked away from him. I went over to reassure her it was okay, although I wasn't sure it was. Lomen's mood had turned so suddenly I wondered if he expected the Witch to hurt us.

I couldn't hear her approach, since she'd taken off her shoes. But I could smell her. Frogwater and dried blood and moldy fabric, all covered with an overpowering sense of gloom. She was a walking bad mood.

"Owww!" she raged as she swept into the room. Her dirty shawl billowed back behind her like it was always being blown by the wind. A wind created by her own fury. "He fried to kite me," she roared.

"Excuse me, Your Royal Witchiness?" the lickloe asked her politely, bowing so low his beak nearly touched the floor. "I didn't quite get that."

"Be cried to site we," the Witch insisted, pacing in frustration.

Lomen glanced sideways at me. "I have the hardest time understanding her sometimes," he said out of the side of his mouth.

I nodded in sympathy.

"I'm sorry, Your Supreme Nastiness," Lomen apologized again. "My ears are slow to understand your powerful superhuman speech."

This was really an insult from Lomen, telling the Witch she talked just about as poorly as a human did. But, being too much like a human herself, the Witch didn't get it. I had to bite my tongue so I wouldn't laugh and give it away.

She turned around and said very slowly, "He tried to bike me."

"Does she mean *bite*?" I asked softly.

"I think so," Lomen whispered. Then he went closer to the Witch. "Who tried to bite you, Your Ultimate Wickedness?"

"That lion!" she insisted. "When I went to harness him to my chariot, he roared and tried to kite off my fred."

Lomen looked at me. "Kite off my fred?"

"I think she means 'bite off my head,'" I suggested.

"Oh. Thanks." He turned back to the Witch. "I'm sorry, Your Ultra-Meaniness. That must have been awful."

"He's my prisoner!" she roared. "He plant bike me."

This time I did laugh. I couldn't help it. She thought she was so powerful and impressive, and yet she couldn't even say the simplest things without screwing up.

Dorothy smiled, too, even though she had no idea what was going on. I guess she was just smiling at me.

But the Witch thought she was smiling at her. Or rather, laughing at her.

"Think that's fudgy, do you?" The Witch swept over to Dorothy and slapped her hard across the face with her long bony hand.

Dorothy cried out in surprise as she staggered back against the wall.

"I won't let something make fudge of me!" the Witch screamed.

Dorothy started to cry, and I have to say the thought of witch-flavored candy made *me* want to cry, too. But I was not as bad off as Dorothy. She was so scared the smell of her fear made my head ache.

I wanted to bike that Witch myself.

But I didn't think it would do any good. If I did, I would be put in some kind of cage, helpless just like Big Cat was.

There had to be another way to deal with her Royal Witchiness. I just had to figure out what it was.

Chapter 21

The Witch refused to feed Big Cat because he wouldn't pull that chariot thing she had. Here in Oz, no one seems to have a car, so I guess if you don't want to walk or be carried by a smelly flying monkey, you have to get someone to pull you in a wagon or something. The chariot only had two wheels, so it looked like it might be real fast on the brick road. But it would tip over easily.

I understood why Big Cat refused to pull it, but personally, I think he should have agreed then crashed her into a wall. Of course, as usual, he didn't listen to me, so he just ended up making the Witch mad at him.

Late that night, after the Witch had gone to bed, Dorothy and I snuck some food into his cage. She squeezed through the bars to get inside.

"Is that you, Dorothy?" he asked in a cautious whisper as he sat up.

"Yes," she answered. "We brought you some dinner."

He gave a low growl and looked around. "Thanks, but you shouldn't have. It's too something."

"But you need food," she insisted. "I must bring it if I can."

I just looked at her. Not once, in all the years I've known her, did she ever say that to me. Yet here she was pledging to bring eternal food to some cat that was practically a stranger.

He hugged her, and they jabbered nonsense talk for hours, pretty much ignoring me. I felt like we were caged up in the one of the animal pens at the State Fair, but without the wonderful smells of hotdogs, roasted corn and cotton candy. I hadn't smelled anything even remotely like decent food since we'd arrived at this castle. What I wouldn't give to be back at the Kansas State Fair! Or even back at the Shiny City, with the ham and biscuits! I hoped Happy and the other wolves were enjoying all the people food. But I hoped they'd leave some for us in case we ever made it back there.

Eventually, I fell asleep and dreamed that Happy and his friends were riding on a Ferris wheel.

I don't know how long I slept, but when I woke up, it was still dark out. Only a thin sliver of moon peered out from behind the clouds, so it was hard to see. But I could hear something. Something besides the snoring of Big Cat.

Dorothy was curled up close to him for warmth, and she seemed to be sleeping soundly. So, the sound that awakened me probably hadn't come from her.

Then, I heard the creak of a rusty metal hinge. It screeched just for a moment then stopped. The clouds slowly pulled away to reveal more of the moon, and in the growing light, I could see someone standing by the door to Big Cat's cage. Someone wearing billowing hooded robes. The wind shifted, and her smell was unmistakable.

The Witch!

She didn't say anything or move any closer. I realized then the moonlight that made it possible for me to see her also made it possible for her to see us. And she could see that Big Cat, who'd tried to "bike her fred off," was just a few feet away. Between her and Dorothy.

I think she had hoped to sneak the shoes away from Dorothy while she slept. But with Dorothy snuggled so close to the cat, she would risk waking him if she tried to take the shoes. We know what would happen then. Her fred would be biked right off.

There was another creak as she slowly pulled the cage door closed. Then, she disappeared silently into the night.

I couldn't sleep anymore after that, even though I moved as close to Big Cat as possible.

The next morning, Dorothy shook me awake as soon as it was light. I mean, she thought she was shaking me awake. Of course, I was already awake, since I'd stayed up the rest of the night on guard in case the Witch came back.

I checked to be sure the shiny shoes were still safely on Dorothy's feet. I mean, I knew they were, of course, since I'd been awake all night. But I had to check, just to be professional. We dogs take our guard jobs very seriously.

We hurried back to the kitchen to wait for orders for the day. Lomen came in shortly after we arrived and set Dorothy to work making cockroach porridge.

Lomen was chopping up fish guts with a short, dull knife. While he worked, he was chewing on something that looked like a baby frog.

"So, I, uh, guess you lickloes don't have to cook breakfast for yourselves, do you?" I asked, a little nauseated. Frogs have never smelled very appealing to me, and a raw one would be really gummy.

Lomen nodded. "Another reason why we are superior to creatures like your human. Your girl has to eat cooked food, just like the Witch."

I decided not to mention that I had developed a taste for cooked food myself.

"Do you have any pork chops around, by any chance?" I asked hopefully.

Lomen opened a dusty cabinet in the back of the room. "I think a pig ear is about the closest thing we have."

"I'll take it," I said. Yeah, they look gross, but they really do taste a lot like a dried-out pork chop. At least, they do when you're as hungry as I was.

Dorothy had only a few dried berries left in her pocket to eat. I offered her part of the pig ear, and Lomen offered her half of a bloodworm, but she shook her head no.

After the Witch's breakfast was cooked, Lomen put it on a battered metal tray and carried it out to the room where the witch ate her meals. In ordinary castles, the room would be called the dining hall, but I'm not sure you can call it "dining" when you're eating boiled ferret faces. Anyway, Lomen soon came hurrying back with his beak pointed downward in a big frown.

"The Witch wants Dorothy to serve her breakfast," he huffed.

"Do you know why?" I asked, but I had a pretty good idea.

"No." He shook out his mane, obviously upset. "She's never asked for a prisoner to serve her before. It's always been my job."

"Don't worry. It's not you. It's the shoes," I explained. "The Witch wants Dorothy's shoes, and she's probably going to keep Dorothy with her as much as possible so she doesn't miss a chance to take them away."

"Why can't the Witch just order Dorothy to give the shoes to her?" he asked.

I shook my head. "I don't know. They must have some kind of special magic power that lets Dorothy resist her."

"Magic shoes?" Lomen sniffed derisively. "I've never heard of such a thing."

I nodded. "I said the same thing about flying monkeys. No, I smelled those shoes. They're pretty powerful, all right. And they came off the feet of another witch, I think. So, I'm guessing they're shoes that give special power to witches. And I don't think we want the Witch to have any more special powers, do we?"

"Of course, we do."

I looked at him in disbelief. "We do?"

"Yes. The Witch is the ultimate in evil. The supreme Goddess of Gross. The most powerful being in all of Oz."

He said all this in such a ridiculous fawning voice I almost thought he must be making fun of her. But his face was quite serious.

Then I remembered. The Witch could see and hear everything he did.

And everything *he* saw *me* do.

"Yeah," I pretended to agree. "I guess she should have the shoes, then."

Then I turned away with a sigh. I would never know whether the lickloe was on our side or not.

After she ate, the Witch followed Dorothy back to the kitchen and watched from the corner while her prisoner washed the dishes. Then she ordered her to scrub the floor.

So, Dorothy filled the bucket from the pump, took the ratty old mop from behind the door and started to swab like a pirate who'd been threatened with walking the plank. But the Witch didn't seem to like the way she was doing it. I wondered if she was supposed to use her tongue or something.

"You should bean there," she yelled, pointing to a spot in the middle of the floor. Dorothy had started in one corner and was working her way along the wall. But the Witch obviously wanted her to do the middle of the floor first.

We soon found out why. As she crossed to the middle of the room, Dorothy tripped over something, and the Witch cackled with glee. So she had hidden something and wanted Dorothy to trip over it. And she wasn't doing it just to be mean.

Dorothy's shoe had caught on whatever the Witch had put there, maybe something sticky or something with a hook. When her shoe got stuck, Dorothy tumbled over, and her foot came out of the shoe. Before either of us had time to react, the Witch had jumped over, snatched the shoe and shoved it onto her own bony foot.

Rats! Now she had one of the magic shoes! Would that make her able to control our minds?

I thought real hard to see if I had the urge to obey anyone.

Nope. I guess she had to have both shoes for that to work.

"You stole my shoe!" Dorothy howled in anguish, and the Witch just laughed, doing a little dance with her prize. The foot with the shoe made clomping noises on the stone floor, and her bare foot just made soft clicking noises as her toes cracked. She looked really stupid, gloating over her silly shoe.

Then I noticed something very odd. There was a strange puddle on the floor around her bare foot. The Witch had danced onto a wet part of the floor, and when her foot rested in a puddle, her heel seemed to sink into the floor. Dark ooze surrounded it, spreading into the water.

It looked as if the Witch's foot was *melting*.

Would water make her melt? Was that why she never took a bath?

I ran over to the bucket and nudged it toward the Witch, hoping I could get it in her way so she would step in it. For a moment, I almost got her. I had pushed it closer and closer, and she was so busy dancing she didn't notice. Just as she was about to knock into it, and at least spill some of it on herself, she saw it and jumped away.

There was a look of fear in her eyes.

I knew it for certain, then. She was as scared of a bath as I was. Even more so, probably. Maybe water wouldn't make her melt all the way, but it would at least slow her down.

"Dorothy," I barked. "Get her wet. Then she'll get all melty and we can get away."

But Dorothy just ran to the corner, crying about the shoe, and curled up into a ball.

With one last look at the bucket, the Witch hurried away.

I wanted to tell someone what I'd discovered. But who could I tell? If I told Lomen, the Witch would realize I knew her secret. I'd tried to tell Dorothy, and she didn't understand.

We would stop this witch. We could melt her with water.

Or at least, I could. It looked like I was going to have to do it alone.

Chapter 22

From that moment on, I was obsessed. I had to get the Witch wet. I just had to.

But how?

She came into the kitchen when Dorothy washed the lunch dishes, but she always took care to stay on the other side of the room, away from the water pump. I tried to show Dorothy that she needed to fill a bowl with water and throw it at the witch, but she thought I was trying to tell her I was thirsty. She put a bowl of water down on the floor for me instead. I started to push it over toward the Witch, but Dorothy just said, "No, Toto. You're making a mess." And she picked up the water and poured it down the drain.

In the afternoon, the Witch gave Dorothy chores to do out in the yard. I was sure she was trying to trip her again, so I ran around barking and nipping at the Witch's heels. If that second shoe came off, she was going to find her foot in my teeth instead of in the magic shoe.

But the Witch shooed me away.

"Get away, dog," she hollered. Then she turned on Dorothy. "Control your dog or I will."

And then Dorothy did something she's never done before.

She tied me up.

Me!

Her best friend.

Her protector.

She tied me to a torch holder on the outer wall of the castle, on the far side of the lickloes' bunkhouse. Then she turned away and went back to work.

I've never been so humiliated in my whole life. Humans don't tie up their best friends, do they? They tie up the cows. They lock up the chickens. But the smart creatures like me are supposed to roam free.

What did this mean? Did she not love me anymore?

I wasn't worried about being too far away to protect her, since I could chew through the rope and run back to her in a matter of minutes. But why should I bother? Why protect someone who didn't seem to want my help?

I moped around feeling this way until the shadows grew so long I figured Dorothy would be heading back to the kitchen to help with dinner. Soon, they would head indoors, and I could get free, slink into the kitchen, hide under the work table, and probably no one would notice me.

Then I realized I *wanted* them to stay outside a little longer. The outer castle wall had a flat part at the top where the lickloe guards walked around, looking out into the woods and fields beyond the moat. Anyone on that was high above anyone in the yard. Including the Witch. I could go up there and drip water on her from above. She'd probably be half-melted before she even noticed!

I quickly gnawed through the rope attached to my collar and took off, looking for stairs up onto the top of the wall. It felt good to run after all that time tied up, and it felt especially good to have a reason to run. I had a plan. And the witch was going to walk right into it.

As I had hoped, there were water troughs for the lickloes up on top of the wall. There were only two, but they were low enough I could reach them, and that was the important part. So, I had water. And I had the Witch in view.

I just had to get the water over to the witch.

It would have been a lot easier with that bowl I'd had in the kitchen, but there wasn't time to go back down to look for it now. The Witch would be finished in the yard any minute.

I didn't have a way to carry any water. All I could do was maybe dip my tail in the trough and let my hair trap as much liquid as possible.

It turned out there was a problem with that plan. That water was *cold*! And I'll tell you—you won't know this if you don't have one—that a tail is not a part of you that likes to get cold all of a sudden. So, I couldn't help myself. As soon as my tail came out of that icy water, I shook to get as much out as I could. Which was exactly the wrong thing to do, because then I had nothing to drip on the witch.

I tried again. And again, I couldn't keep from shaking the water off.

But the fourth time, I focused really hard. I thought of my girl, and how I needed to save her. So, before I could shake, I ran.

I ran around the top of the wall, dodging curious lickloes and trying to keep my tail up so all the water wouldn't drip off onto the ground. By the time I reached the place where I would be standing over the Witch, I was completely out of breath.

But it was worth it. She was still there, making Dorothy sweep up loose gravel and trying to trip her so she would lose her other shoe. Dorothy had no other shoes to wear, so she was walking around with one foot just in a sock, and it probably really hurt to walk on the stones. The Witch had one bare foot, too, but I didn't care if the stones hurt her. This was her castle and those were her stones, and if they hurt it was her fault. She shouldn't be trying to steal people's shoes.

Once again I was struck with a really strong urge to bite her, even though she would probably leave a super-nasty taste in my mouth. But I didn't want her to notice me while I dripped the deadly water on her.

When I was standing directly above her, I turned around, stuck out my tail and wiggled a bit to encourage it to drip. I didn't want to shake, because then all the water would just end up on the castle wall. The problem was, the Witch was moving around too much, and it was hard to keep track of her because I had my tail in her direction instead of my head. In other words, I couldn't see what I was doing. There were some good-sized drops in the beginning, but they were all wasted because they hit gravel instead of witch. I had to focus.

But it wasn't working. Before long, I was out of water, and the Witch wasn't melting. Not the tiniest bit.

I had failed.

The Witch pushed Dorothy back toward the kitchen. I wouldn't have the chance to try again. I wanted to howl, I was so frustrated. Instead, I knew I had to go to the kitchen and find another way to get the Witch wet before she found a way to steal Dorothy's other shoe.

Chapter 23

*D*odging the paws of the lickloes guarding the wall, I ran to the stairs as fast as I could. I had a new idea, and this one would work. Since the water in the troughs had been too cold for me to get really wet, I would try the water in the moat. It had to be warmer. Then I could get all the way wet and shake off on the Witch while she was watching Dorothy in the kitchen.

I was pretty out of breath by the time I found the opening in the outer wall. I stopped to pant a little and take a look around. Then, I kind-of wished I'd kept running.

The opening in the wall led directly to an old wooden drawbridge. I'd hoped I could run down the bank to get to the moat, but there was no bank, only flat, steep stone walls going straight down into the churning dark water. So much water!

To get down to the edge without jumping in, I would have to run across the bridge, climb down the bank on the opposite side then run all the way back And I would have to do all that without being noticed by the two lickoes standing guard at the bottom of the drawbridge.

I needed something to distract them. A rat would be terrific, but I didn't see, hear or smell any of them around. Maybe a nice fat dragonfly...but I didn't see any of those, either.

I bent low toward the ground.

"I hear the bugs here are really fast," I said into the dirt, hoping someone would hear.

"We grlurgh are," a voice answered almost immediately. "We outrun lickloes every day."

I searched through the gravel and dirt to find whoever had spoken but couldn't see anyone.

"I don't believe it," I said, hoping I could trick him into proving his claim. "Lickloes are too fast."

"If I wasn't faster, I wouldn't still be here," the voice answered.

"I can't tell if you *are* here," I replied. "I can't even see you. For all I know, you're the ghost of a bug that wasn't quite fast enough."

"I'm fast grlurgh enough."

Right before my eyes, an enormous earwig tunneled up out of the ground, proudly wiggling its curved antennae.

"Maybe," I allowed. "You can tunnel fast, but can you run? Out in the open where the lickloes can see you?"

"Do it all the time," he bragged.

This was just what I'd hoped for. A bragging bug.

"Okay, prove it," I challenged him. "Run out there in front of those guards."

"That's too glurgh easy," the bug insisted. "I'll climb up the wall and outrun the lickloes up there at the top."

Well, that would do me no good whatsoever. I guess I'd made him brag a little too much.

"I can see you better down here," I pointed out. "If you run up onto the wall, I might not be able to tell it's you."

"Bad eyesight, huh?" the bug said as it smoothed its antennae. "Alright, then. I'll run down here. But be sure to watch."

"I will," I promised, even though I was already focusing on the end of the drawbridge.

"Watch me, now, here I go!" the bug bellowed as he charged past the guards.

As soon as the guards started to chase him to the left side of the drawbridge, I took off down the right side. The planking was dry and rotten, so splinters jabbed up into my paws. But soon I reached the end and looked for a way down to the water.

"Watch me!" the bug screamed.

"I am," I lied.

"No, you're not," he insisted. "Watch me!"

"Okay," I barked, annoyed.

I turned to see the earwig as it danced a few steps of the can-can on the edge of the bridge. One of the lickloe guards snapped his beak just inches from the bug's head.

"Nice," I called, hoping he could avoid being eaten before I finished my errand.

There was no path down to the churning river. I would have to climb down through the rocks. Dog paws are good for many things, but climbing really isn't one of them. Paws full of splinters are especially bad for climbing. And the dark water moved so fast, I was afraid I would stumble, fall into the moat and be swept away.

You know I wasn't, though, because otherwise I couldn't be here telling you this story.

Anyway, I was scared. But I made myself get closer and closer, step-by-step. Finally, I was close enough to step into the water and get myself wet. This was the moment I'd been waiting for.

"Watch me!" the earwig yelled from up on the bridge.

"Yeah, you look great," I hollered back as I stared at the water rushing by just inches from my nose, trying to figure out how to get some on me without getting too wet.

"How would you know? You're not even looking!" he screamed.

"I looked really fast. So fast you probably didn't even see me look."

"Oh, yeah?" the earwig challenged. "Then tell me what I'm doing."

"You're annoying me," I muttered.

"Look, look! You'll never see something like this again," he insisted.

By now, I didn't even care if he succeeded in distracting the lickloes. I just wanted them to eat him and shut him up.

Staring at the water wasn't making me feel any better, though, so I finally decided I would give in and make him happy. I looked up to see the earwig spinning and howling, almost like he was breakdancing. On top of a lickloe's head. The other lickloe kept trying to chomp on the crazed bug, but I guess his partner didn't want to risk getting his head pecked, so he kept dodging out of the way.

I had to admit, it actually was pretty funny.

But it wasn't solving my problem, which consisted of about eight million gallons of treacherous, swirling water. I had to get some on my hair to carry it back to the witch. I knew from experience that dipping my tail in the water was probably not going to work, since it would make me shake. So, I decided to try a paw. Maybe the water would wash out a few splinters.

I crept even closer to the roaring moat. The sound of rushing water pounded through my head. I could feel mist on my face, and it smelled like every bath I had ever had, all here at one time and place. But for Dorothy, I could do it. I could get wet.

Slowly, carefully, I reached out my left front paw. At first, I felt nothing. Then I realized I wasn't actually touching the water yet. I got closer.

Instantly, icy water yanked me forward, pulling like the arms of a giant sea monster. A huge-acious, ginormous, very strong and very wet sea monster.

I knew right then this wasn't going to work. By the time I got in deep enough to get a good amount of water in my hair, I would be pulled down into the swirling moat. Then I'd be no help to Dorothy at all.

I would have to try something else.

I turned and started to scramble back up the slippery rocks toward the drawbridge.

Coward!

Who said that? Did I say it to myself?

You're afraid of the water.

I am not. It was just too dangerous. It was moving too fast.

You didn't really even try because you hate water so much.

So? What if I am afraid? I'm still right about the "being swept away" part

Maybe.

Oh, great. Now I didn't just have to fight a wicked witch and a castle full of lickloes, I also had to fight some strange voice in my head.

"Look at me!" the earwig yelled triumphantly as I scurried up onto the drawbridge. I did, and saw him jumping from the head of one lickloe to the other.

The next second they ate him.

"Thanks for trying," I barked as I ran by, hoping to get back into the castle before the guards noticed me.

"You're welcome," he answered as he tumbled through the air. Apparently, the guards had started fighting over him, and in the scuffle, he slipped out of their beaks. The moment he hit the bridge, he disappeared between the rough planks.

So, I guess he had been right about his speed and bravery. I hate it when annoying people are right.

I hoped the annoying voice in my head wasn't right about me being a coward. I had seen cowardly behavior from Big Cat, and I've gotta say, it was kind-of embarrassing.

I made it back inside the castle walls while the lickloes were clawing at the surface of the bridge, trying to reach the brave earwig. From there, I ran for the kitchen like a mad—well, you-know-what.

I ran furiously, as if I had a plan and were desperate to put it into action. But I wasn't. I mean, I *was* desperate, but I didn't have a plan and I wasn't in a hurry to do something because I didn't know what to do. I think I just ran to keep myself from thinking.

What *could* I do? Even now, the Witch might already have managed to get the second shoe. She'd become all-powerful, probably. We'd never be allowed to leave. She might even take over the world, or at least this strange corner of the world.

I had to *do* something!

But while water seemed to be everywhere, it wasn't near enough to the Witch. I wasn't having much luck getting the water on her, so I would have to get some help. The Witch was too frightened of Big Cat to let him near her. Dorothy and the lickloes were the only ones close enough to do the job. Obviously, her lickloe slaves weren't going to help me melt their master, since she could read their minds. So, I needed to get Dorothy to do it.

But how could I make her understand?

Chapter 24

I slowed to a trot as I got nearer to the kitchen. There was no need to hurry. I still didn't have a plan.

I changed to a walk. I walked slower and slower, but I still eventually reached the kitchen, where I would have enacted my brilliant plan, if I'd had one.

To my great relief, I saw that Dorothy was still wearing the remaining shoe as she stood in front of the fire stirring something that smelled like toasted toenails in a pan. She was safe, for the moment. The Witch sat on a rickety stool nearby, her gaze following Dorothy's every movement.

The water bucket was on the other side of the room. If only I were taller, like a Rottweiler. Then I could probably carry the whole bucket over and splash her. Of course, if I was a Rottweiler, I would be big enough to just eat the Witch and wouldn't have to bother trying to melt her.

But I am not a Rottweiler.

I sighed.

After the cold, damp outside air, the warmth in the kitchen felt wonderful. So, despite the weird aroma of frog livers cooking on the rotisserie, I moved closer to the fire and lay down to rest.

I'm embarrassed to say that I fell asleep, right there in the middle of the biggest crisis of my whole canine existence. I know I fell asleep because I dreamed I was a Rottweiler. But when I bit off the Witch's head, two new heads appeared in its place. She cackled with laughter in stereo. I ripped off her arm and she grew four more. So, even a big vicious Rottweiler couldn't defeat the witch.

I dreamed next that I pushed her into the fire, but instead of burning up, she just glowed like a hot horseshoe. With an evil grin, she reached out with her long, skinny, red-hot fingers to grab Dorothy and burn her arm.

I jumped forward to stop her, and that's when I realized I had been dreaming. When I looked around, the Witch wasn't glowing and she wasn't reaching to scorch Dorothy. She was still sitting on her stool. Waiting.

And watching. As if she had hidden another object she expected Dorothy to trip over at any moment.

I glanced at the water bucket so far away. Then, I glanced back at the non-glowing witch. Maybe I *could* burn her. But what if fire made her stronger? I knew water could hurt her, so fire might actually help her.

What if I set the Witch's dress on fire? Being the nice person she is, Dorothy would pick up the water bucket and douse her to put the fire out.

Wouldn't she?

But what if she didn't? What if she wasn't actually nice enough to help a wicked witch? I mean, I sure wouldn't. If Dorothy didn't put out the fire, then it might make the witch stronger.

Of course, Dorothy would put out her *own* dress if it were on fire. But that wouldn't get water on the Witch.

I kept thinking. Would she put out me if I were on fire? Creepy thought, since I don't wear a dress. I'd have to set my hair on fire.

Or maybe not. Maybe I could just pick up something that was burning, and she'd put the fire out to keep me safe. Assuming she noticed. If she didn't notice, then my hair probably *would* catch on fire.

I'd need to have lots of fire, so there'd be lots of water. If this plan worked, I would get completely soaked and possibly drown in melted witch ooze. But as I looked at Dorothy, shaking with fear while she cooked the witch's dinner, I knew it would be worth it. I could save my girl.

Slowly, I got up and crept over to the woodbox. The kindling had all fallen to the bottom, of course. I tried not to make too much noise as I rooted through the box to pick up a few pieces that would catch fire quickly.

"Your dog is making a dress," the Witch growled, looking over at me.

"Toto," Dorothy called in a weak voice. "Move away."

I dragged a couple of sticks over to a dark corner and waited until the Witch stopped paying attention to me and went back to staring at Dorothy's shoe. It didn't take too long. Humans have a short attention span. Then I took my sticks over to the fire and tried to casually dangle them near the flames.

It wasn't easy looking casual while doing this, especially when Dorothy shooed me away again.

I gave up trying to avoid attention and decided instead to attract as much as possible. I stuck the sticks right into the fire, lit them and ran straight for the Witch, growling as loud as I could. The hem of her long ragged gown began to smolder as I held the burning stick up to it.

But it wasn't catching fire.

"Get your dog away!" the Witch yelled to Dorothy, paying no attention whatsoever to her smoldering dress.

Dorothy started crying, and she wasn't paying any attention to the dress, either, or to the burning sticks in my mouth that were getting shorter and shorter by the second. I smelled something like burnt hair and hoped it was the Witch's gown, but from the heat on my face, I was afraid what I smelled was me starting to singe.

I had to drop the fire. But if I dropped it, Dorothy would never reach for the water. So, I held on.

And then, the fire finally caught on the edge of the Witch's gown.

"Oh!" Dorothy screamed, pointing toward the flames. "Fire! Fire!"

She looked around and sighted the water bucket. Just to be sure the Witch would get wet, I kept a tight hold on the burning sticks and moved even closer to her. It seemed to take forever, but at long last, Dorothy doused us both with a thunderous splash of cold water.

The Witch screamed, a sound so high and so piercing it made my head explode with pain. I couldn't tell whether I'd dropped the burning sticks. My vision grew blurry as the horrid shrieks echoed through my head. There was a smell I can only describe as melted frog, even though I've never seen or smelled a melted frog.

And then there was nothing.

Big Cat was out of his cage, letting
Dorothy ride him like a horse.

Chapter 25

When I woke up, Dorothy was holding me and crying. My fur smelled really bad, and it hurt to move. But despite all that, I felt great. Because I was sure the Witch was gone.

There was a pool of melted sludge that smelled unmistakably like frog water and baked dandruff, but it was more than that. I knew the Witch was gone because I could *feel* that she was gone. The sense of awful gloom that had hung over everything in the castle was starting to fade like smoke in the wind. My plan had succeeded; the witch was gone.

When Dorothy realized I was awake, she hugged me close, which was very sweet except that it hurt a lot. I licked her hand, but everything tasted like sour cinders so I didn't keep that up for too long. I was so happy and yet so tired I couldn't decide whether to wag my tail or curl up and go to sleep. Tail-wagging is usually not something I have to decide to do—it just happens. But this time, sleep happened instead.

I woke up the next time feeling stiff but not hurting as much. Either I had sleepwalked into the yard or Dorothy had carried me there. Lickloes were dancing around a bonfire, making squawking noises they probably thought was singing. It sounded awful, but at least it was a happy sort of awful. Big Cat was out of his cage, letting Dorothy ride him like a horse. She was wearing both of the shiny shoes again, so I guess she must have taken the one back from the witch, or what was left of her.

I could smell cooking food—real food, not the nasty combinations of things the witch ate. Pork chops? Maybe. Or steak. Or chicken. Or some unknown meat that tasted like all three. The wonderful aroma made my mouth water, and I wondered if maybe somehow we'd all gone to heaven.

It was great just to watch Dorothy as she smiled and laughed. I could feel the relief radiating from her like sunbeams through the window on a winter afternoon. She must have been so frightened of the witch—and now she was free. We were all free.

The lickloes squawked about freedom, and running through the fields and something that seemed to involve putting blackberries between their toes. I didn't ask. Everyone was happy, and that was all that mattered.

Well, I was actually not as happy as it seemed like I should be. We were safe. We had food. And yet, something didn't feel right. As Big Cat pranced by in time with the music, I realized what the problem was.

While we were here, partying and having a great time, the others who'd made the journey with us were lying out in the cold, broken and alone. Strawman had had his guts pulled out by the flying monkeys, and Metal Man had been dropped down a deep ravine. They would never be able to join us.

Unless they had some help.

I wasn't sure why I cared, really. Strawman had tried to feed me by putting food in my ear, after all.

And Metal Man had this annoying squeak when he walked that really got on my nerves.

I tried to focus on those annoying things and not think about how they'd helped us get through the woods and how they'd cheered Dorothy when she was sad.

It didn't work. I still felt guilty.

But what could I do? I couldn't even reach a pork chop on a table. How could I reach down into a horrifically deep ravine to help Metal Man get out? And while I love my paws, they aren't much use for putting stuffing back into things. I wanted to help our friends. But what could I do?

Even the smell of roasting meat couldn't cheer me up. And later on, after we'd all eaten and Dorothy and Big Cat sat by the fire talking, I could tell they were starting to feel it, too. The guilt.

The lickloes didn't feel guilty, of course. They just kept squawking about how they were free of the "most evil smellypants." I couldn't blame them for being happy, but it didn't help us at all. I wanted to ask if they had any ideas about how to rescue our friends, and they were all busy putting berries between their toes.

If only we had wings, like those smelly monkeys, we could fly over and pull out Metal Man.

Lickloes had beaks, so they should have had wings, too. But they didn't.

It was the monkeys' fault. They tore up Strawman. They should put him back together. And I'd tell them, too, if they hadn't all flown away.

Then I remembered what Lomen had told me about the monkeys. The Witch had called them to do three tasks by using the special hat. If I could get Dorothy to put the hat on...

But I couldn't tell her what she needed to do with the hat. If I brought it to her, she'd just think I was chewing on it.

What would happen if *I* put the hat on? Could I call the monkeys?

There was only one way to find out.

The stairs leading to the Witch's room were much steeper than I remembered. It took me forever to get up there.

But even though all I could see was one stone step after another, there was a smell of dead things that told me I was getting close. Fortunately, the Witch didn't believe in shutting her door very tightly. I was able to push it open without smashing my nose too much.

The hat was right where I'd last seen it, on a shelf not far off the ground. However, though the shelf was near the floor, I was much nearer. That shelf was just out of my reach. I'd have to jump for it.

I was soooo glad that none of animals back in Kansas could see me now. Here I was, jumping like a silly rabbit, trying to snag something I couldn't even eat.

When I finally managed to grab the hat, it tasted just as dusty and dry as it looked. Not that I tried to eat it, but I did have to pull it down with my mouth, after all. Then once I had it, I had to decide what to do with it. What if I called the monkeys, and they couldn't understand me? Well, then they'd leave. That wouldn't be so bad, just a little embarrassing. I stuck my ear inside the hat and barked.

Nothing happened.

Okay, maybe that didn't mean anything. After all, the monkeys could fly, but they couldn't get here between one minute and the next. If they were coming, I'd have to wait a while for them.

If I had to wait, I might as well sleep.

Chattering woke me up. Even before I could see them, I could hear the noise. How could they possibly have that much to say to each other? I swear they were worse than chickens.

Then I could smell them, a combination of coarse hair, musk and bananas. They were definitely coming.

"I'm in here," I barked. I might as well see whether the monkeys would listen to me.

"E-e-a-a-oh. Didja hear somethin', Matty?" a monkey voice asked from outside the window.

"Sounded small," Matty answered in an equally annoying monkey voice. "E-e-a-a-oh. Like a rodent."

"I'm not a rodent," I barked indignantly.

"E-e-a-a-ooh. I can't see anythin.'"

"I'm here. On the floor," I called when I could see the shape of a flying hairy thing in the window. "Look down."

It really hurt my pride to say that, but otherwise I figured they'd fly on and offer their services to the lickloes. Then the monkeys would probably be sent off to hunt for more berries for the lickloes' toes instead of rescuing our friends.

"Oh, there you are," the monkey said as he stuck his ugly head through the window.

"Do ya see it, Matilda?" the other monkey asked.

The first monkey, who apparently was not called Matty because of smelly matted hair but because *her* name was Matilda, pointed toward me.

"That's it, Fleaflit."

"I'm a him, not an it," I barked. "And you have to do three tasks for me."

Matty rolled her eyes.

The other monkey, Fleaflit, curled his-or-her ugly lip into a sneer.

"What'ja say? You said you want us to go back home? Sure, right away."

"Ha-ha, nice try," I barked. I decided I'd better issue orders pretty soon before they tried to leave. "Okay, listen. You need to take me and Dorothy and Big Cat back home, and you have to pick up Metal Man and Strawman on the way."

"That's two things," Matty said with a snort.

"Well, I get three things, don't I?" I answered quickly.

"The little rat's got a point," Fleaflit said, casting a sour look at the hat on the floor.

"So, that's settled, then." I barked as I moved over to sit on the hat. "You collect my friends and take us all home. And if you can do it fast enough, I'll give you this hat back so no one else can order you around."

That got their attention. The sneer on Matty's face turned to a blank look of astonishment.

"Ooh-oh-ah. You'd really do that?"

"You bet," I barked. What did I have to lose? If the monkeys took us home, we'd be back in Kansas where magic hats probably wouldn't work and flying monkeys would most likely be mistaken for large ugly geese and shot out of the sky during hunting season. So, that hat wouldn't be much use to anyone I knew.

Fleaflit patted me on the back. "Little rat, you're alright."

"I am a *dog*," I said, gritting my teeth.

"I meant it as a compliment."

"Would you like it if I called you a..." I tried to think of something insulting. "A little human?"

Fleaflit shook his (or her) head. "E-e-a-a-oh-ugh, no."

"Then just call me a dog. Or," I said slyly, "you can call me 'Boss.'"

So, that's what they did.

It was great. Matty and Fleaflit commanded a whole squadron of flying monkeys who all called me "Boss" as they swooped down to pick up an astonished

Dorothy and Big Cat. They carried us back over miles of dark woods, obeying my every command.

And the whole time Dorothy just thought I was barking at them.

Chapter 26

The monkeys could sort-of talk to Big Cat, so they let him know they were taking us to find Metal Man. Then Big Cat could tell Dorothy so she wasn't worried. She didn't understand I was in charge. Humans are kind of dense sometimes.

It was near sunset by the time we'd collected Metal Man and the monkeys had put Strawman back together. We still had a long way to fly to return our metal friend to his woods and the straw guy to his cornfield. After that, who knew how long it would take to get all the way to Kansas? So, I decided we'd better find a place to make camp for the night.

"We're going to stop in that clearing over there," I told Matty, who was carrying me in the front of the formation. "We'll set up some soft places to sleep and then get something to eat before we rest."

"Okay, Boss. Ya mean that clearing right there?"

Matty dived toward a tiny open space barely large enough for an anorexic cow. My stomach lurched up into my throat.

"No!"

"How about this one?" She zoomed over a tall tree with long needles then raced down the other side, hurtling toward the ground at breakneck speed. I think she was trying to make me sick, and it was working.

"No, you nearsighted nitwit," I said, gasping for breath. "The big clearing that has enough room for all of us to land."

By now, we were practically right over it.

"E-e-ah-oh. That clearing there, ya mean?" She nodded toward the open space but didn't drop any lower.

"Yes." I barked. "We land there."

"Right there?"

"Yes."

"Right there on that sharp rock?"

"What rock?"

I knew Matty was stalling for time, and I had a pretty good idea why.

She shrugged. "We're past it now."

"Yes, and now we've almost passed the entire clearing." I pointed out, annoyed.

"Then..." She grinned at me. "...we'd better stop quick, right?"

Before I could answer, she turned and, with a cackle of glee, dove like a falling rocket straight for the ground. She may have enjoyed the thrill, but I didn't have as much faith in her flying and landing skills as she seemed to. I was so sick I was ready to throw up the dinner I hadn't even eaten yet.

I took several deep breaths as the rest of the group landed nearby, and then gathered all my strength so I could give the next set of orders without fainting.

"We're setting up camp here for the night," I barked in a weak voice. "Make up beds then get out whatever food rations you have."

"E-e-a-a-oh. Let's take *him* apart again," Fleaflit suggested as he reached for Strawman.

"What?" I barked when I saw what he was about to do. "No, no, you can*not* use my friend's straw to make a bed. Go find some leaves or something."

The monkeys all grumbled, but they did as ordered. Fortunately, the dense forest provided a lot of dry leaves and things that looked like Christmas tree needles but smelled like cow poo. They were happy enough with that, and no one else threatened to use Strawman for a bed.

Once the sun disappeared behind the heavy canopy of trees, it grew dark fast. After my nausea went away, though, the forest no longer had the oppressive gloomy feel it'd had when we were first there. The Witch's castle still loomed in the distance, but it now was witch-less and run by berry-stomping lickloes.

"Can you find something to eat besides bananas?" I asked after the monkeys had made up beds for everyone.

"E-e-a-a-oh. Why?" Matty asked. She held out a backpack and showed me it was full of bananas. "We have enough."

"You have too many," I corrected her. The bananas were all squished together and gave off the sickening-sweet aroma of overripe, bruised fruit. "Some of us would like meat for dinner."

Matty looked down her nose at me. "Ya should become a vegetarian. It's much healthier and better for the planet."

"Listen, Banana Breath," I answered, "First, I am a carnivore. I eat meat. Second, if I look unhealthy, it's because I just had a rancid witch melt all over me and then went flying with an out-of-control monkey who never should have had wings to begin with. And third, I don't even know what planet we're *on* right now, so I don't really care whether my dinner is good for it or not."

She sighed.

"Well, okay. But meat gives ya bad breath."

"I'm a dog," I barked. "I'm gonna have dog breath no matter what I eat."

"Okay," she grumbled. "There's a stream over there. I'll pick up some fish."

Not my favorite, but I was really afraid I'd be stuck with bananas or straw for dinner, so I nodded.

"Fish will be fine. Get one of your guys to build us a fire to cook it."

She looked down her nose at me again.

"Real carnivores eat raw meat."

I gave her the same look in return. "You really don't want me to give you that magic hat back, do you?"

"Okay, I'm going."

She gave a series of whistled commands and was soon joined by two of her other monkeys. They flew off over the trees. Others began to gather wood and tinder for the fire.

My work here was done for the night.

I went over to the woodpile, selected a nice stick and settled down for some serious chewing. Dorothy came over, and for a moment, I was afraid she was going to start throwing sticks around like she does at home. Fortunately, she got distracted by a hole in Strawman's shirt. He was leaking stuffing out the back, so she tried to find a way to patch the hole.

I had a good chew while the last traces of light disappeared from the west and the sky darkened to a deep velvet black.

"I'm gonna miss these nice sticks when we get home tomorrow," I said to Fleaflit as he came over to supervise the monkeys tending the fire.

"Ya don't have sticks? E-e-a-a-oh." He rubbed his tail thoughtfully between his fingers. "Do the humans burn them all?"

"They probably would if they had any," I admitted. "No, we don't have many sticks in Kansas because we don't have many trees. Just a lot of grass."

"Kansas?" Fleaflit seemed so confused he dropped his tail into the fire. "Ye-e-a-ow!"

"You shouldn't do that," I suggested.

He blew on his tail, which didn't look or smell the least bit burnt.

"I've never heard of Kansas."

"Best place in the world," I answered.

I never stopped to think about whether it was true or not, I just said it. Kansas was home, and that made it the best place for Dorothy and me.

"Well, that's nice," the monkey answered slowly, "but if I've never heard of it, then I don't know where it is."

"Look on a map or something," I barked a little impatiently. I was starting to get worried. I wasn't sure how far we had to go, but it was a long way; and the monkeys might pretend they couldn't fly there because they didn't know where it was.

Fleaflit snorted.

"I don't need a map. I could navigate around all of Oz even with my eyes closed."

"But our home isn't in Oz," I pointed out.

"Well, that explains it, then." He began to rub his tail again.

"Explains what?"

"Why I don't know where it is," he answered.

"Well, you'd better find it," I ordered, "because you're taking us there tomorrow."

He yawned as his tail uncurled slowly toward the fire.

"No, we're not."

"Yes, you are." I nodded toward the magic hat, which I had put in the pocket of Dorothy's dress. "Remember?"

The monkey turned to me with an ugly grin.

"The hat only works in Oz, Little Rat" His teeth glowed dully in the firelight.

That's what I had been afraid of, but up until that moment, I hadn't really allowed myself to think about it. Could we be lucky enough that Kansas was somewhere in Oz?

I looked at the overgrown cat standing on his two hind legs while he spoke human language with a guy made out of a giant can, and a talking bag of straw. No, Kansas was not part of this weird place.

"Fine," I said at last, anxious to get the smug grin off Fleaflit's face. "But you have to take us as close to Kansas as possible."

"But since I don't know where Kansas is, I don't know what part of Oz is closest to it." He flung his tail down in frustration, just barely missing the fire.

"Not my problem," I said as I picked up my stick and started chewing again.

"E-e-a-a-oh!" He began to pace anxiously around the fire. "We could fly around for days and never know if we're close or not. We'll be exhausted. We'll run out of bananas!"

"Then maybe you'd better find a map," I repeated.

"E-e-a-a-oh! Of course!" He danced in a grotesque little circle, looking very much like, well, a monkey. "The Wizard!"

"He has a lot of bananas?" I asked.

"No, ya idiot." Fleaflit gave a funny little leap. "The Wizard will know how to get close to Kansas."

I dropped my stick and sat up. The dopey monkey might just have come up with the answer to our problem of how to get home.

"Who is this Wizard? Where do you find him?"

The monkey's lip curled up into a massive ugly sneer.

"Ya don't know who the Wizard is?"

"No, I do. I just thought I'd pretend I didn't so you could sneer at me," I answered.

"Ha-ha-a-a-oh-oh." Fleaflit danced and starting chanting in a singsong voice. "Little Rat doesn't know the Wizard. Little Rat doesn't know the Wizard."

"Why did I even bother?" I muttered.

"The Wizard is only the most magical being in Emerald City, that's all," the monkey said, gloating in my face.

"Oh, well, I don't know where Emerald City is, either," I answered, pretending to yawn.

"E-e-a-ha-ha!" he cackled. "The city of shining emeralds that glitters so bright ya can see it for miles! And the little rat has never seen it!"

Did he mean that shiny city where people wore things over their eyes to protect them from the glare? Since about all we'd seen in Oz, other than that city, was corn and trees, I figured the shiny city had to be this Emerald City he was talking about.

That meant the big Fathead must be the Wizard, whatever that was. If they were all like him, then wizards were pretty useless. I didn't like that guy at all. He'd smelled worse than anything we'd met so far. Like sandwich scraps that had been left in Dorothy's lunchbox too long—they seemed okay at first, but when you got close enough to take a bite...ugh.

So, he was the most powerful magical being in the only city in this whole place? I didn't like it, but we might have to try to get help from him, even though his magic was probably no better than the guy who pulled rabbits out of a hat at the state fair.

"Do you think he'll know how to get all the way to Kansas?" I asked carefully.

"Not my problem," the monkey said, still sneering. "We just have to get ya to the edge of Oz." He started doing his little dance again.

I took my stick and walked around to the other side of the fire. If I never saw another monkey again it would be too soon.

When Matty flew back with the fish, I told her to tell Big Cat we would be flying to the shiny city in the morning to see the Wizard. After I was finished making all the travel arrangements, I headed over to take care of Dorothy.

She hugged me and fed me a big piece of fish. It had prickly bones that stuck in the back of my throat, but I didn't care. I could feel the happiness radiating from my pet girl. She smelled like rainwater on a dusty, dry day. Even her voice seemed to be smiling as she chatted in the mindless human way with Strawman, Metal Man and Big Cat. I guess they thought the Wizard in the shiny city was going to take care of all our problems. I wasn't so sure. But I did remember there was wonderful food in the shiny city.

If the wolves hadn't eaten it all.

Chapter 27

Monkey breath is worst in the morning. The monkey who carried me (after I refused to ride with Matty again) had dried banana crusted around the edge of his mouth, but his breath smelled way worse than bananas. It was like he'd been eating breakfast with a witch. I had to turn my head away from him the whole time we were flying, which meant I was staring down at the ground as we rushed over trees and fields with frightening speed. Well, not *frightening* speed. I wasn't scared or anything. Just a little dizzy.

There wasn't a whole lot to look at. Ugly dark treetops. Fields of ugly dark grass. Even the sensation of wind in my nose wasn't enough to make it interesting. But after hours and hours of this monotony, I could finally see the outline of the shiny city on the horizon. So, it wouldn't be too much longer.

The monkeys saw it, too. They started to chatter about where they were going to go out to lunch after they got rid of us. For a moment, I really hoped the wolves *had* eaten all the food, just so the monkeys would be disappointed.

But I don't think wolves eat bananas.

I was not looking forward to seeing the Fiery Fathead again, but if he could get us back to Kansas, it would be worth it. So, I was anxious to get to the city to get the meeting over with. It seemed to take forever to get there.

The scenery below gradually began to change. There were fewer trees and more fields and some of those smelly flowers. Then, all at once, we were over the field full of the flowers that had made us all sleepy. The monkey who was holding me started to yawn, so I kicked him in the ribs to make sure he stayed awake. We hadn't come all this way just so the he could take a nap.

The city still seemed far away, but some buildings became distinct. My mouth watered at the thought of the ham and other great food that was there waiting for us, and I kicked the monkey again to try to hurry him up.

But then I saw something a little odd, and I wanted him to slow down so I could get a better look. I felt a little sick when I realized what it was.

In the fields full of sleepy flowers below, a wolf lay curled up asleep. That would be one of the wolves we'd sent on to the shiny city days ago. He'd been asleep all this time, probably, and would stay that way until he starved to death.

It made me a little sick because it had been my idea for them to travel this way, and I hadn't warned them about the fields. So now this poor wolf was doomed to sleep himself to death because of my advice.

Unless we stopped to pick him up.

We could take him with us to the shiny city. Suddenly, I knew what I had to do.

"Stop!" I ordered the monkey.

"E-e-ah-huh?" He looked down at me, breathing a big blast of foul breath in my face, but his wings didn't miss a beat.

"We need to stop," I explained slowly, so his slow monkey-brain could understand.

He shook his head. "Not unless Matty says."

"Hey, Matty!" I barked loudly. "Tell your monkeys we need to stop!"

She flew closer to us. "Ya want something, Little Rat?"

"Yes," I growled, ignoring the rat comment. "We need to stop and go back to pick up that wolf." I nodded toward the flower fields behind us.

She flashed a grin that was not at all friendly.

"Sure, we can go back." With a whistle, she waved her arms, and all the monkeys executed a sharp turn. I was concerned about that smile and whether it meant something bad, but the sudden turn and our quick descent to the ground made me nauseous again, so I forgot about it.

"What's happening?" Dorothy called out as the monkeys deposited her on the ground.

"We shouldn't stop in this dangerous field," Strawman insisted.

Metal Man and Big Cat started complaining, too, but since I couldn't explain what we needed to do, I just had to let them whine for a while.

After my monkey and I landed with a heavy thud, I jumped out of the his arms to run over to the wolf. I guess I wanted to make sure he was still alive. I didn't need to worry—I could hear him snoring right away. As I got closer, I recognized Happy.

"Wake up!" I barked.

He continued to snore.

I nudged him with my nose, but he didn't seem to be any closer to waking up. I turned back to Matty.

"Never mind," I barked. "We'll just take him asleep and wake him up when we get there."

"Do with him whatever ya want," she said with that fake sweet smile.

"Pick him up, then."

"Oh, no." Her smile grew broader. "Ya told us to turn around and stop here."

"Yes," I said impatiently. "And now I'm telling you to pick him up and continue on to the city."

"But we followed your order to stop." Her grin widened. "That was your third order. We don't have to do what ya say anymore."

"Yeah," the monkey who'd been carrying me grumbled. "And your first order was really more like about twenty-seven orders anyway." He reached back to scratch his butt.

I rolled my eyes. "Technically, you're correct. But then, I don't have to give you back the magic hat, either."

"Ya can't use it again." Matty said smugly.

"Oh? Okay, fine. I'll have someone else use it."

I said it with confidence, but secretly this worried me a lot. Since Dorothy and the others didn't understand me, I couldn't explain to them what to do with the hat. They were still whining and waiting for the monkeys to pick them up again. Instead, all the monkeys started to fly away. Without us.

Big Cat roared in frustration, and Strawman tried to catch one of them by making his rope belt into a lasso. A good idea, but the monkeys were already out of reach.

I brought Dorothy the magic hat, hoping she might realize she could call the monkeys back, but she just stuck the hat in her basket and waved me away. So, I took it back and ran over to Happy. Somehow, I had to wake him up.

I barked in his ear, but it made no difference. I tried to push him, but I'm embarrassed to admit I was too small to accomplish anything.

This was making me mad. I had stopped to help him, and he was making things impossible for me. So,

I bit him. It probably wasn't the nicest thing to do, but I thought pain might be the only way to force him awake.

He chuckled in his sleep.

I bit him again, a little harder this time, and he laughed again. Apparently, instead of hurting him, I was tickling him.

I climbed up on his back and jumped up and down. He laughed again, and one eye opened for a moment. It looked like I was going to have to tickle him awake.

It was a little humiliating, but eventually, it worked. I ran up and down his back, jumping and wiggling my toes, until finally he convulsed with laughter and rolled over, sending me sprawling into the flowers.

I got up and pulled the hat onto his head.

"Call the monkeys back," I barked.

"L-like, what?" he said groggily.

"Monkeys," I repeated. "Call the monkeys."

"Money?"

I thought about it for a moment.

"That's probably close enough."

I looked out at the monkeys flying in the distance, and sure enough, they started to turn around as if they'd heard the command from the magic hat.

"Ha! We did it." I turned back to Happy and found he was asleep again.

"Wake up!" I jumped onto his back

I think he actually snored.

"Come on!" I barked into his ear. "You need to wake up to tell the monkeys to carry us to the shiny city."

There was another snore, more distinct this time. How could I get him to tell the monkeys what to do if he wouldn't wake up? The answer was, I couldn't. So,

I would just have to pretend he was the one giving the orders.

Before the monkeys got close enough to see, I crawled down into the grass behind Happy's head and pulled the hat over me. Soon, I heard the annoying chatter of monkeys. I took some satisfaction from the fact they seemed as annoyed with us as we were with them. After a minute, I heard something land nearby with a soft thud.

"Ee-aa-oh. Who called us this time?" Matty snapped.

Happy snored.

I stuck my paws under his head to make it move a little.

"I did," I barked, trying to disguise my voice.

It sounded like another monkey landed on the other side of us.

"Whatta they waa-ahheant this time?" Fleaflit whined.

"I dunno," Matty answered impatiently. "I don't even know who called us."

"That wolf's wearing the hat," Fleaflit pointed out.

"Yeah," Matty snorted, "but he's asleep."

"I am not," I squeaked. Okay, so my disguised voice sounded more like a field mouse than a wolf. It wasn't as if I'd had much time to practice.

"Did he say something?" Fleaflit asked.

Happy snored.

"Ya see?" Matty kicked him with a creepy monkey foot that looked like a hand. "He's snoring. That means he's asleep."

"I just have a sinus condition," I squeaked. "Take me up in the air away from these flowers, and my voice will get better." I figured that, once he was away from the poisonous flowers, Happy would wake up; and then he could give the rest of the orders. I wondered if I would start getting sleepy myself. But I think I was too annoyed to fall asleep.

"Okay," Matty snapped. "That's one order. Take him away, Fleaflit."

Uh-oh. We were going to end up separated at this rate.

"Take all the others, too." I squeaked.

"Ee-ah-ha!" Matty laughed. "That's two orders. Ya only get one more."

I thought about how much effort it might take to get Happy to understand what that last order had to be. Instead of asking to see the Wizard, he'd probably ask for a chicken gizzard or a barbecued lizard.

So, just before Fleaflit hoisted Happy into the air and revealed me hiding in the grass, I barked, "Take us all to see the Wizard."

"That's three!" Matty shouted in triumph as she flew off. "That's all you're going to get."

And that's all we need, I said to myself as a monkey scooped me up into his arms. *At least, I hope it is.*

Chapter 28

The shiny city didn't look as shiny as it had last time we were there, maybe because it was a cloudy day. So, I didn't have to keep focused on the ground, and no one tried to put funny glasses on me.

The monkeys flew right to the People Palace where we'd met the Fiery Fathead, or I guess I should say "the Wizard." I didn't really believe he was powerful enough to get us back to Kansas, but, as the monkeys said, he might at least know where Kansas *was*. Then we'd find a way to get there, maybe by using the Witch's magic stick.

After he woke up, Happy had told me a lot more about that stick, which Dorothy now carried in her basket, the stick the Fiery Fathead had shown her in a vision. I think she was planning to give it to the Wizard, but I wasn't sure that was a good idea. He would just keep it and do magic for himself. We might need that magic to get home.

We also needed to keep Happy with us for a while so he could tell me more about how that magic worked. I promised him that if he stayed with us, there would be a feast with ham and other delicious people food, so he agreed.

At the door of the palace, the guards with the pitchforks stepped aside when Dorothy held up one of the shiny shoes, just like before. Some of the monkeys began to fly away over the city walls as Dorothy and the others started inside. I held back. There was something I needed to do—I just wasn't sure I wanted to do it.

But a promise is a promise, even if it's made to someone who calls you a little rat.

"Matty, wait," I barked just as she was crouching for take-off. I jumped up and pulled the hat off Happy's head.

"Hey," the wolf protested. "Like, what're you doin' with my souvenir witch hat?"

"I'll get you a souvenir witch stick instead," I promised him. Then I turned to Matty. "Take the hat."

She looked at me incredulously. "D'ye mean it? We didn't take ya home."

"You took us as far as you were able." I nudged the hat with my paw. "And it doesn't seem fair that other creatures can order you around just because they're wearing this silly thing."

"Ya got that right," she agreed. "I hate being ordered around. I wake up in a bad mood every day just thinking about it."

I nodded. "It shows."

"Yeah." She grinned sheepishly as she picked up the hat. "Well, maybe now I won't be in such a bad mood."

"Just one thing, though," I insisted.

"What?" she asked.

I gave her my sternest look. "Don't ever refer to a canine as a little rodent."

She grinned. "I won't, little wolf. Or rather, I should say, little friend. You've been a great help to us. When we tell the tale of how we were freed from the cruel magic of the hat, we will tell about your kindness and bravery."

I shook my head. "No, you won't. You'll just ask each other where you can find more bananas."

"Yeah," she admitted with a snort of laughter. "You're probably right. We talk about food a lot."

"That's okay." I wasn't really sure I wanted monkeys chattering about my bravery and kindness. It would just make the world a more annoying place.

"Thank you," she said as she tucked the hat under her arm.

"Any time." But I didn't mean it. There wasn't going to be another time because we would be leaving this place soon.

I turned to run after Dorothy and the others. I'd assumed they would be going to that big room where we had met the Fiery Fathead, but they were so nervous and excited, they'd moved their mouths more than their feet. So, it was pretty easy to catch up to them.

Happy was running, distracted, from one side of the hallway to the other, slipping on the polished floor tiles and careening into the walls.

"I smell bacon!" he yapped gleefully. "And over here—ham and eggs."

I smiled smugly. "I told you, didn't I?"

"Yeah, but, like, where *is* the food?" he asked, his excitement fading as he started to look a little confused. "I smell it, but I can't see anything."

I nodded toward one of the closed doors in the hall.

"People are cooking it in the kitchens, and then they serve it to people in other rooms. So, you might be getting the smell from food that's already been moved."

"Aw, man." He rubbed his nose with his paw. "This is torture. When do we eat?"

I looked at the line of closed doors lining the hallway as we headed toward the big set of double doors at the end. Our toenails made little clicking noises as we trotted along behind Dorothy and the others. The smell of food was starting to get to me, too, but I tried not to show it.

"I think before they let us eat we have to talk to the Fiery Fathead. I mean, the Wizard."

Happy grinned. "Dude, you'd better not let him hear you call him a fathead. He'll turn you into a cat or something heinous like that."

I snorted in disdain.

"He can't understand me. He only talks people talk. And besides, I don't think he has enough magic to turn me into anything. I'm beginning to think he sent Dorothy to the Witch to steal her magic stick just because he was too scared to do it himself."

"Wow, that's low, man." Happy shook his head, which made his scraggly fur look even more scraggly. "She's just a pup."

"I know," I agreed. "Everyone seems to think this Wizard is so great and powerful, but people also thought the Witch was powerful, and she couldn't even handle a bath without falling apart. This Wizard probably isn't much better."

Happy stopped. "So, why d'you want to see him, then?"

"We need a way to get home," I admitted. "But I'm thinking maybe that magic stick can do it. Do you know how it works?"

"Yeah, sure. Well, sort of." He looked down at the floor. "Not really. I mean, the Witch used to wave it around a lot, but nothing really happened. So, then she started hitting things with it. That was usually a bad idea."

"Why?" I asked.

"They'd sort-of blow up."

"*Sort-of* blow up?" I wasn't really expecting that. "How can something *sort-of* blow up?"

"Well..." He thought for a moment. "Like, one time she sat down on her broom like it was a horse and she was gonna ride it somewhere. And she waved her stick and nothing happened. So, she banged the stick against the broom handle. I guess she thought she could use magic to get her broom to act like a horse."

"And did it?" I asked hopefully. If the stick made her broom act like a horse, then it must contain powerful magic.

"Well..." Happy rubbed his nose again. "...it threw her off, which is what I would have done if I was a horse and she was sitting on my back. But it didn't just throw her, it sort of exploded up into the air and blasted her along with it."

I thought about that. "Maybe that's what she wanted it to do."

He shook his head. "I don't think so. Let's just say, she wasn't real happy when she landed in the lickloes' water trough."

"Oh." I thought about it some more while we ambled along to catch up to the others. They had stopped at the end of the hall to wait outside the room where the Fiery Fathead was hovering over his chair.

That stick definitely had magic power of some kind, but the Witch hadn't been able to control it. Maybe she needed the magic shoes to be able to get the stick to work. Maybe she needed to bang the stick against the shoes.

Maybe, if *we* banged the stick against the shoes, it would blast us back to Kansas.

Then, again, maybe it would just blow us up. Of course, Happy had aid it "sort-of" blew things up. It really sounded more like it just blew them around.

It was worth a try.

I was ready to go home.

So was Dorothy. Although she and the others had been talking and laughing all day, I could still tell she wasn't happy. I could hear the longing in her voice and smell nervousness hanging over her like a fog. She was afraid the Wizard wouldn't be able to send us home, but she pretended to the others that everything would be okay. It was hard to watch her, so after a while, I turned to look at Happy again, who was sniffing and licking under the table where the door attendant had been sitting.

"I wouldn't lick those legs if I were you," I said. "You don't know where they've been."

"Yeah, but it makes my tongue tingle," he said with a slurp.

I shook my head. "You're weird."

"You got anything better to do?"

"No," I admitted.

Now that we'd reached the end of the hall, *no one* seemed to have anything to do. So, we waited. And waited.

Then, just when we'd waited so long I considered giving the table legs a lick myself, the door finally began to creak open. The attendant, a big lumbering human with a heavy face that reminded me of a ham hanging in the smokehouse, waved for us to step inside. He stepped back against the fabric panels along the wall to let us pass, then trudged back outside, leaving us alone.

The big Fathead wasn't fiery when we got to the enormous dark room where he sat, or hung, over his chair. He looked sickly and pale, like he'd been the first time we'd seen him. He still had no body, and no smell, either.

"Why have you come here?" he roared in his self-important voice.

Dorothy, shaking a little from fear, stepped up to his chair.

"We came back because you said you would help us."

"Oh? And just what did I say I would do?" the Fathead drawled.

"Y-you said you would help me get home." She was trying to put on a brave face, but I could tell she was starting to doubt she could trust the Fathead.

Strawman stepped forward to join her in front of the Fathead's chair.

"And you said you would give me trains."

"And me a cart," Metal Man added as he clomped up next to them.

They all turned to look at Big Cat, who was clutching his tail in his hands. Oh, that's right, he'd asked for courage. He'd shown some back when we were dealing with the Witch, who was dangerous, and yet now that all he had to face was this pathetic hovering Fathead who was so weak he'd sent a twelve-year-old girl to fight his battles for him, he was more cowardly than I'd ever seen him. *He* needed brains, in my opinion. They all needed them.

And speech therapy.

"Why should I help you?" the Fathead demanded.

"We killed the Witch," Strawman explained.

"Did you?" He sounded like he didn't believe it. "How?"

Metal Man put his arm around Dorothy, who was still trembling.

"Dorothy melted her with a bucket of water."

The Fathead snorted in disbelief.

"You expect me to believe that something story?" His voice was so loud we all jumped back a bit in surprise.

Then Big Cat stepped forward.

"Yeah, we do," he growled. "Got a problem with that?"

"We can prove it," Strawman added. "We have her something."

At his urging, Dorothy reached into her basket to pull out the Witch's magic stick.

Oh, no! She was going to hand it over to the Fathead Wizard right now, before I had a chance to find out how it worked.

I calmed down a little when I realized she couldn't hand it to him because he didn't have any hands.

"Okay," I whispered to Happy. "I think they're just about done, and then it should be time for the banquet."

But whatever the Fathead said next didn't involve a banquet or anything else that any of us wanted.

"I'll have to think about it," he said. "Let me keep the something overnight, and then come back tomorrow."

"No!" Big Cat roared.

"You've had enough time to think," Strawman argued.

"We did what you ordered us to do," Metal Man added.

Dorothy had started crying and wasn't able to say anything.

"Listen, people," the Fathead bellowed, "I said tomorrow!"

I could feel his words rumbling through the floors.

That shut everyone up.

"Now, give me the something," the Fathead insisted.

Slowly, bent over like Auntem's old mother, Dorothy shuffled forward and set the Witch's magic stick on the Fathead's chair. Strawman put his arm around her shoulders as she stepped back, and they all turned and started to leave.

That was it?

No banquet?

No return home?

We were just going to *leave*?

I couldn't believe it.

Well, we weren't going without the magic stick. I'd find out how to use the Witch's magic to take us home even if it took me the rest of my life. Before anyone could stop me, I ran up to the chair, jumped up and grabbed the stick.

Chapter 29

Well, okay, it took three tries to reach it, but I managed to snag the stick and take off before anyone could stop me.

"Toto!" Dorothy admonished. "Bring that back."

No way. Not after all those times I had to fetch her sticks for her. This time, I was keeping it.

I banged it on the floor to see what would happen. It scratched the marble a little but, other than that... nothing.

Dorothy ran toward me from one side, and Big Cat came toward me from the other. Everyone was yelling, not that I paid enough attention to understand them. I had to find the secret to the magic before someone took the stick away.

I ran over to Happy.

"Rhat roo I roo rith it?" I barked out of the corner of my mouth. "Row roes it rork?"

"Bang it on a broomstick, man," he suggested.

"I ron't rav a roomstick," I called over my shoulder as I dodged Metal Man and headed for the corner.

"Bang it on that magic hat, then," Happy barked. "Twice the magic equals...um..well, a lot more magic."

Of course! He was right. Two magical objects would be more powerful than one. But I'd given the magic hat back to the monkeys. Had I given away our only chance of going home?

I slowed down so much Strawman almost caught me against the wall. Then I remembered the shoes. I turned sharply so that, instead of grabbing me, Strawman grabbed a handful of the fabric panel hanging on the wall. I ran straight for Dorothy. Since I would probably only have one chance to do this, I had to get it right.

I dashed up to her, scooted to a stop and smacked the magic stick against the magic shoes. Immediately, there was a flash of light so bright I had to close my eyes. I heard a roar and was propelled backwards through the air. It was working! The stick was blasting us back to Kansas!

But when I landed, I realized that either Kansas smelled a lot like the Wizard's room, or the magic hadn't worked. I was tangled up in something that was definitely not Kansas prairie grass. It was more like a shower curtain. I must have been blasted under the fabric wall panel.

I wasn't the only one. There was a short, fat human with no fur on his head. He smelled old, and his round face looked familiar.

"Toto?" Dorothy cried in a voice full of anguish.

"I'm back here," I barked to let her know I hadn't returned to Kansas without her.

The human backed away. I could smell his fear.

Why was he scared of me? He was so much bigger, he could have just sat on me and there wouldn't be a whole lot I could do about it. If he was frightened, I must have looked pretty fierce.

Or maybe he had done something wrong and knew he was going to be punished.

I growled to see what he would do. Cowering, he lurched back into some kind of machine.

"Toto!" he yelped. "Get away!"

How did this strange guy know my name? I growled again. It wasn't fair that he knew who I was when I didn't have the least idea who he was.

"Eeh!" He squealed like a dog standing in front of a full bathtub. "Don't hurt me, Toto!" he yelled. He was pressed back as far as he could go. I expected him to lunge for the side.

Instead, he turned his head and spoke into a metal stick, saying "Toto!" in a voice so loud it made my skull echo. It was just as loud as the voice the Fathead had used to get everyone to stop arguing a few minutes before. And now that I thought of it, this bald human kind of looked like the big Fathead, too. Were they related?

They didn't smell the same. This guy smelled like sweat and fear and potato chips, and the big Fathead didn't smell like anything at all. Like he wasn't even there.

Could the big Fathead be just a picture of the fat head of this guy here, speaking into a magic stick to make his voice loud?

Suddenly, there was a ripping sound, and Metal Man's axe tore through the fabric panel just above me. Then everyone was jabbering at once.

"Who are you?" Strawman demanded.

"Where is the Wizard?" Dorothy asked.

The bald fat guy hung his head.

"I *am* the Wizard," he said meekly.

"I don't believe it," Strawman said, looking around as if he expected to find the Wizard hiding behind the fat guy.

Metal Man raised his axe.

"I hope you didn't try to hurt Toto."

"Hey, do you have potato chips back here?" That was Big Cat, who obviously hadn't learned to focus yet.

"Guys," I barked, "I think the fat guy is telling the truth. I think he *is* the Wizard."

"It was all me, but I had some help from something." The little man walked over to the big chair and pointed at the ceiling, where there were mirrors and machines. I guess he used the devices to make it look like his head was floating above the chair. No magic was involved. He probably didn't know any more how to use the Witch's magic stick than I did.

But he did know how to make pictures appear on the wall behind the chair. He drew one on a little screen then hit a button, and it appeared on the wall. So, that was how he'd made the picture of the Witch and the stick. He may not have been much of a wizard, but he was a pretty darn good artist. With a few strokes of a pen, he created very vivid images.

Then, he drew a picture of something else.

"Look, man," Happy licked his lips as he looked up. "It's a giant ice cream cone."

I shook my head.

"I don't think so. The bottom is too flat. It looks more like a basket."

"Naw, it's an ice cream cone," Happy insisted. "I saw them at a fair when I was a cub. And right there in the middle, it's got lots of chocolate sprinkles."

"Those aren't chocolate sprinkles," I said, moving closer to get a better look. "I think they're people."

Happy shrugged. "People, sprinkles—they're all good on ice cream."

"Stop that," I hissed. "You're supposed to be a pet. Nice and cuddly and safe."

"And hungry," he pointed out.

I nudged him toward the corner, in case there was someone around who could understand me.

"You will get more from people," I whispered, "if you act cute instead of mean."

"Oh, okay." He looked at the picture on the wall one more time. "But where *is* the food?"

As if on cue, the Not-Really-a-Wizard stepped away from his picture machine and stepped over to a door near the chair.

"You all have many questions," he said with a smile, "but something something answers much easier on a full stomach. Let us celebrate the something something something occasion with a feast."

I couldn't catch all of the words, but I got the most important one at the end. I nodded to Happy as we took the Not-Really-a-Wizard up on his invitation.

"Don't let him out of your sight."

The Not-Really-a-Wizard threw the door open with a grand gesture. My jaw nearly hit the floor. Where the room we were in was dark and cold, the one beyond radiated heat and light. The smell of roast pork, buttered potatoes and baked beans rushed out with such force it set our noses twitching. Well, Strawman's nose didn't twitch because it's fake, and Metal Man's nose probably can't move enough to twitch and he doesn't eat roast pork, anyway. But you get the idea.

The banquet tasted as good as it smelled. There was even ice cream for dessert, so I wondered if maybe Happy was right after all. The picture the Not-Really-a-Wizard had drawn was probably just a picture of what we would be having for dessert, not a picture of random people standing in a basket under a round blob.

After the feast, I curled up in the corner—the corner farthest away from Happy because he snores—and went to sleep. When I woke up, it was dark and ghostly smells were all that remained of the heavenly feast.

There were two open doors, and I figured one of them would lead to Dorothy. I sniffed at the first one, but even before the aroma of cat hair hit my nostrils, I heard snoring that definitely did not come from my Dorothy. I could smell straw and oil, too. So, the three wise guys were in that room.

At the other doorway, I caught a whiff of sunshine and prairie clover. That was the right one. I trotted inside, sniffed my way over to the bed, then clawed my way up the bedspread to get to the top. Back at home, Dorothy always left a pile of books next to her bed so that I could climb up any time I wanted, but I guess she didn't have enough books to do that here.

Or maybe she forgot.

I tried not to think about that. Lately, she'd been so busy talking to her new friends, and I'd been so busy talking to Happy, that I hadn't spent much time playing with my girl at all. I wondered if she liked being with her new friends better. Did she want to stay here with them, and live in the People Palace with the Not-Really-a-Wizard? Did I want to? There was plenty of delicious food, and the beds were soft and warm, and no one tried to hit me with a pitchfork just because I dug a little hole in her garden.

But this place wasn't home.

Could we bring our new friends back to Kansas with us? Metal Man could help with the farm work, and Strawman would scare the living daylights out of the crows. But the wolf and the six-foot-tall cat would be a problem. Auntem might have a heart attack, and Unclehenry would have his gun out and start shooting so fast the neighbors would think the country was under attack. So, no, we couldn't take our new friends back to Kansas.

I snuggled up against my girl, but it took me a long time to fall asleep.

I had to get those other shoes!

Chapter 30

When I woke again, it was morning. Sunlight streamed through big, wide, shiny windowpanes, and Dorothy was standing in front of a tall mirror, twirling in a dress that smelled new but looked pretty much like the one she'd been wearing. One of the workers brought in a bowl of stew for me and some oatmeal for Dorothy, and we took care of the most important meal of the day.

Then I decided it was time for a nap on the bed while some workers in big poofy dresses came in to fuss with Dorothy's hair. The next thing I knew, I was being lifted in poofy-sleeved arms.

I smelled something horrible, worse than the nervous body odor of the Not-Really-a-Wizard or even the stink of the Witch's bony foot. It was a bath—a steaming expanse of water decked with soap bubbles. And the the big poofy sleeves were about to lower me into it.

No way!

I clawed up to a shoulder and ran down a back. Maybe Dorothy wanted to get all fixed up and pretty—I think she even *likes* getting a bath—but I didn't want one, I didn't need one, and I wasn't having one. Period. I got wet saving her from the Witch, and that was enough for the year. I still had nightmares about the feeling of water everywhere, even in my nose. Baths were nasty things.

Okay, I admit it. They're not just nasty, they're scary. I'm always afraid my skin will never feel dry and normal again. I'm afraid my hair will lie matted in wet clumps against cold slimy skin forever. So, when I jumped off the back of the lady with the poofy sleeves, I wasn't taking any chances. I ran under Dorothy's bed and stayed there until they were gone. In fact, I stayed there even *after* they were gone.

It was only when Dorothy was starting to leave that I decided to come out. I didn't want to get left behind. Not that I was afraid she would forget me or anything...

Well, yeah, to tell the truth, I was afraid she would. When she opened the door, I darted out with her, and she looked down.

"Oh, there you are, you bad dog." But she smiled, so I knew she didn't mean it.

We joined up with Big Cat, Strawman and Metal Man out in the hallway, and I barked a few times to tell Happy that, wherever he was and whatever he was chasing, he should stop and come help us.

Something was about to happen, but I had no idea what it was. I could smell the excitement and sense of anticipation radiating from Dorothy, as though she were a pie fresh from the oven. She thought we were going home.

I wasn't so sure. Especially not if she was relying on the Not-Really-a-Wizard.

There were more people in the hallway than I'd seen before, and everyone was babbling and excited, and lots of people were patting Dorothy on the head as if she were their pet girl and not mine. The crowds got thicker the closer we came to the door, but there was still no sign of Happy. I was afraid he hadn't heard me call.

Then, just as we were about to leave the palace, he dashed out from a side hallway and skidded into me. His breath smelled like tacos.

"Where did you find the...?" I started to ask. "Never mind. It's too late for me to go back, anyway. Look, I need you to keep your ears open and your nose to the ground. This Not-Really-a-Wizard guy is up to something, and it could be disastrous."

"Yeah." He nodded. "Like, you'll probably all lose your hair."

"Lose my hair?" I'd been thinking of being blasted to pieces or burnt to a crisp. I hadn't given a thought to hair loss.

He wiggled his ears.

"The guy's, like, totally bald, dude. You could end up just like him."

"I'm not too worried." Unclehenry was pretty darn hairless, and it hadn't ever affected me. But I don't think Happy knew much about humans.

Outside, it was hard to keep from reeling at all the smells. There were people odors—sweat and emotions—and with so many of them crowded in the street, even the smell of their wool coats and leather shoes was nearly overpowering. To my left, I could smell meat pies, but we hurried past that aroma and came to other women selling food from baskets they carried on their arms. There were bread, fruit and fried cheese, just to name a few. Happy started drooling right away. I kept having to nip him on the hind leg to keep him from chasing those baskets.

Then, I had to almost run to keep up with Dorothy. People pressed in on all sides, and I was afraid of being stepped on. Voices and laughter echoed off the buildings that lined the narrow streets. It was so closed-in I couldn't figure out why anyone would willingly live there when there was so much open space outside the city walls.

I still couldn't tell where we were going, but a smell that started faint and kept growing stronger told me we were approaching water.

If all of these people worked together, they could probably get me into a bath no matter how hard I tried to dodge it. I sure hoped that thought didn't occur to any of them.

After a while, we reached a place where the sounds didn't echo as much—we were in an open space like a farmyard. There were no animals other than cats and mice, which I ignored. Once you've chased a chicken, other animals aren't worth the effort, if you ask me.

Anyway, the smell of water got really strong as we approached a low stone wall. I couldn't hear any sounds of rushing, like with a stream or river or toilet. I couldn't see anything, like a lake or pond. I jumped up on the wall to get a better look.

That was a mistake. I nearly fell into a huge-normous bathtub made of stone. Water stretched out before me like a giant mirror with reflections rippling gently across the surface. It was mostly one reflection. One big reflection that took up almost all the space in that stone pool.

The reflection of a giant ice cream cone.

But it wasn't a giant ice cream cone, of course. If it had been, I would have been able to smell the ice cream as soon as I came out of the palace. No, it was just something roughly the same shape as an ice cream cone but not made out of food.

Very carefully, I ran around the edge of the stone wall to see the object reflected in the water. Dorothy and the others were going toward the ice cream-cone-thing, too, so I wasn't worried about losing them.

As I got closer, I could see that the flat-bottomed ice cream cone was just a big wicker basket, like Auntem used for clothes. It was attached by leather straps to the ice cream part, which didn't look at all like ice cream up close. It smelled like hot glue. And it didn't act like ice cream, either. Someone was holding the end of it over a fire, and if they tried that with ice cream, it sure wouldn't be hanging up in the air like that.

No, the ice-cream-cone-thing that the Not-Really-a-Wizard had drawn for Dorothy turned out to be a balloon. She would have known what it was right away, since she understood more of his words and we had seen balloons at the county fair. People paid to take rides up in the air. I'd hoped some of them wouldn't come back, but they always did. They'd rise up, and float for a while, and then come down in a field at the edge of the fairgrounds.

So, it looked like the Not-Really-a-Wizard planned to take us back to Kansas in a balloon. That would work real well as long as Kansas was about two hundred yards away.

But it wasn't. We'd flown on raging storm winds for hours to reach this strange land, and we weren't going to be able to get back by floating on a gentle breeze for fifteen minutes. We'd just end up in a ravine somewhere with a bunch of monkeys laughing at us.

The balloon wasn't the answer. We needed magic—like the shoes and the witch stick. I didn't know what the hairless guy had done with the stick, but Dorothy at least had the shoes, and we could use those.

The crowd started to thin out a little near the balloon, and a moment later, Dorothy and the Not-Really-a-Wizard led the rest of the group up to the basket, which was big enough to hold maybe two of them. If they all tried to fit in, the bottom would break out.

Dorothy turned and threw her arms around Strawman in a big hug, which made him wobble a little.

"I will miss you," she said a little tearfully.

Okay, it looked like they weren't going to try to squeeze everyone into that basket. Probably just Dorothy and me and the Not-Really-a-Wizard.

They all started hugging and talking fast the way humans do when they say goodbye. Dogs are a little more laid-back about these things.

Happy nodded toward the balloon.

"You going in that thing?"

"I guess." I looked out over the crowd—the people and their cats and a few wolf-dogs on leashes. Then I turned back to Happy. "Leave them some food, okay?"

"Sure, dude." He laughed. "Hey, man, thanks for everything."

"You, too."

He turned and strolled toward a woman with a basket of sandwiches while I headed over to join my girl. We were going home.

Chapter 31

Dorothy scooped me up while she was still talking to Strawman. They hugged again, with me squashed in the middle.

Don't worry about me. I don't need to breathe or anything.

Finally, they let go, but before I could catch my breath, she handed me to him.

What? She was leaving me behind?

Oh, okay, she just needed both hands to climb into the balloon basket. Then Strawman handed me back to her. Whew.

Dorothy had to struggle to stay upright, because the basket was lurching from side to side as the balloon tugged on the ropes that held it to the ground. The Not-Really-a-Wizard climbed in after her and started yelling at all the people gathered in the farmyard.

"Good people of Oz," he began in a dull, heavy voice that made it sound like whatever he was going to say had to be boring. "I want to tell you something something something…"

He said a lot of things but probably didn't tell them anything important like "I was a complete phony, and I don't know any magic" or "There are scary creatures outside the city walls, so you'd better feed the wolves well so they will take care of you."

Nope, he probably didn't say anything like that at all. But he sure did talk for a long time.

I started thinking about what we were going to do when the balloon landed and Dorothy realized we hadn't made it anywhere close to Kansas. Since we didn't have the magic stick to bang on the shoes with, maybe we could bang the shoes against each other. All Dorothy would have to do was click her heels together a couple of times.

I looked to see if she was standing with her feet close together. She was—it would have been pretty easy for me to bang the shoes together myself.

Except she wasn't wearing them.

Oh, she was wearing shoes, but they were new, satiny dance slippers made of the same fabric as her new dress. The people who'd brought her the new dress must have given her new shoes to match.

Arghhh! What is it with women and shoes? Why do they always want new ones when the old ones smell so good?

And in this case, the old ones were magic and probably had enough power to take us home.

I had to get those other shoes!

I could have asked Happy to go back for them, but by now he was probably so far away he wouldn't hear me if I barked for him. If I wanted the shoes, I'd have to run back to the palace myself to get them.

I looked up into Dorothy's face, glowing with happiness. She wasn't going to like this at all, and I couldn't explain what I was doing or why. She would just have to trust me.

And I would just have to trust that she wouldn't leave without me.

Taking a deep breath, I hurtled out of her arms, over the side of the basket and hit the graveled street with a heavy thud.

"Toto!" Dorothy shrieked.

I didn't wait for the "something something something." I just ran. I ran along the stone wall as fast as my legs could carry me.

I'd always thought that mixed terriers were the very best kind of dog, but now I wished I was a greyhound with long, slender speedy legs. Instead, I was short, slow and useless. Dorothy would hate me for delaying her. Or worse, she would just leave me behind.

But I had to try. Without the shoes, she'd never make it home.

I kept running. It was hard to squeeze through all the legs of the people and the wheels of their wagons and carts that lined the streets. It was also getting harder to breathe, since I'd been running for so long. But at last I saw the palace up ahead. Since the Not-Really-a-Wizard was also not really living there anymore, someone had left the door wide open. I ran inside.

It wasn't hard to find the shoes—they were sitting on a shelf in the room we'd slept in the night before. And it wasn't hard to get them off the shelf, because it was low and I only had to jump a few times to reach them. Carrying them, however, would not be so easy. If I carried one at a time, I could still run, but I'd have to make two trips. If I carried them both, I would have to walk and I couldn't really see where I was going.

But we needed two shoes, and if I arrived with only one, Dorothy might make me leave without letting me get the other one.

If she hadn't left already.

Opening my mouth as wide as I could, I clamped the edge of one shoe in one side of my mouth and the edge of the other shoe in the other side of my mouth. Then I staggered out of the palace and hoped I could find my way back to Dorothy.

Yes, I know I probably could have tried banging those shoes together and blasting myself to her, but I might have ended up someplace acres away from my girl. So, instead, I tried very hard not to bang the shoes into each other.

I had to walk pretty slowly, so it seemed like it took days to even get back to the point where I could smell the water from that big bathtub with the stone wall around it. There was still a lot of noise from people jabbering, but the noise didn't seem as happy. There was an undercurrent of anger and dismay.

"Hey, man," Happy called from somewhere behind me. "Where'd ya go?"

I had to set down the shoes to answer.

"I went back to the palace. To get these." I nodded toward the witch shoes. Even though it had been a long time since the Witch had worn them, they still left a funny frog-water taste in my mouth.

"Wish I coulda helped," Happy said. "I tried to follow you, but I couldn't squeeze through all the people. I did make one kid drop a bag of cookies, though." He licked his lips.

"Were they good?" I asked, hoping I didn't sound as envious as I felt.

All at once, I felt the nervous excitement that had driven me on for so long starting to wear off. I was hungry and tired and just wanted to curl up and sleep for a while.

He nodded. "Chocolate chip"

"You can't eat too many of those," I warned him. "Chocolate is poisonous to dogs."

"I'm a wolf," he pointed out. "Anyway, if I gotta be poisoned, that's the way I wanna go. Can I help you carry those?" He sniffed at the nearest shoe, and his nose wrinkled immediately in disgust. "Man, I do not miss that woman at all. She was always coming over to her sister's castle. And she'd be, like, all 'my wolves are so much nastier than yours.' And our witch would be, like, starving us more trying to make us meaner. And—"

"Yeah," I interrupted. "I doubt anyone misses either of them. And yes, you can help me. Can you take one of the shoes? I'm trying to get back to Dorothy. If she's still here."

It occurred to me then that Happy could probably tell me whether she'd left yet. Just around the corner up ahead was the open space with the big bathtub and the balloon.

"She's still here," Happy said when I asked. He reached down to pick up the nearest shoe, then paused. "But I gotta warn you—she's in a bad mood."

I held my breath. "Is the balloon still here?"

He shook his head. "That's why she's in a bad mood. You ruined her chance to go home. Everyone out there's been repeating it over and over."

"Over and over?" I winced. "Is that really necessary?"

He shrugged. "Well, you know how bugs are."

Great. Even the beetles running through the cracks were saying bad things about me. If I listened really close, I could probably hear them even now. Not that I wanted to.

"Let's get this over with, then."

I picked up the other shoe and started forward. Now that I knew all the anger and discontentment in the voices on the streets was directed at me, the city felt very dangerous. And when we turned the corner and stepped into the open space, it felt even worse. It didn't just sound worse—I could *feel* the menace toward me. Everyone stepped back away from me as if I had mange.

"Dorothy deserves a better dog," someone growled as I walked past.

"He should be whipped," someone else added.

"Naw," another voice said in disgust. "He should be drowned like an unwanted kitten."

I stumbled, but tried to keep going without looking around to see who'd said that. Up ahead, the sky shone bright and blue...and empty. No balloon.

"A-caw," a bird croaked as it circled above me. "Here's the little rat-dog."

Some birds can understand people-talk, so they were probably the ones who'd told the other animals why Dorothy was mad at me.

"He made the Wizard's girl (a-caw) cry when he ran away," another bird called. "Let's peck his eyes out."

I wanted to explain why I'd run, but I didn't want to put down the shoe. And the birds wouldn't listen to me, anyway—they don't pay attention to anyone without feathers.

Instead, I just hurried faster toward where Dorothy was, or at least where she'd been when I left. It suddenly occurred to me I didn't have any idea where she was now.

I stopped. Happy ran over me and bonked me in the ear with the shoe he was carrying. "What's the matter, man? Why'd ya stop?"

"Do you know where we're going?" I demanded. "Do you know where Dorothy is?"

"No, I guess not." His face contorted in thought for a moment. "I know! You should ask the birds."

"No, I shouldn't ask the birds!" I hissed back. "They just threatened to peck my eyes out."

"Oh, yeah, well, then, maybe not."

I sighed. "I know she's here, somewhere in this crowd. And she probably doesn't want to see me."

By now, I'd figured out what must have happened. When I jumped out of her arms and ran to the palace, she must have climbed out of the balloon to look for me. That balloon had been ready to lift off, so without our weight to hold it down, it probably started to float away. Or maybe the Not-Really-a-Wizard just decided to leave without us. Either way, I was sure Dorothy felt stranded. She probably felt hopeless, too. She didn't know our only real hope was in the smelly shoes Happy and I were carrying.

Or that we had been carrying. We'd both set them down so we could talk, and now Happy was starting to sniff his way over to a pretzel stand, leaving the precious shoe behind.

"Happy!" I barked. "We have a job to do."

I picked up my shoe and waited for him to come back. Then we continued on toward the place where the balloon had been.

Birds occasionally circled overhead, jeering, and that would set off grumbling noises from the people all around us. Really! The people of Oz should thank me for destroying the Witch and exposing that phony Wizard and sending him away. Instead, they were all ready to pull my hair out. I saved the whole country, and this was the thanks I got.

Fortunately, it wasn't too hard to find Dorothy. She was still near where the balloon had been, sitting on the stone wall that surrounded the giant bathtub. She was crying. Her quiet, heartbroken sobs made me hate *myself* for a moment. I could feel the terrible sadness that hung over her like a cloud. She believed she would never get home.

But we'd show her she was wrong, Happy and I. We'd bang the shoes together, and the powerful magic would blast us right back to Kansas.

I trotted up and set the shoe down in front of her. Then I signaled for Happy to come closer and do likewise. Dorothy looked up, her tear-streaked face twisted with anger.

"Toto!"

I didn't need a translation for the "something somethings" that followed. I knew she blamed me for ruining her chance to get home. But I'd surprise her, and we'd be home.

I nodded toward the shoes.

"Okay, Happy. Get right up next to Dorothy, and then bang your shoe against mine."

"Got it." He took the shoe in his mouth.

I took mine. We leaned close to Dorothy, smacked the shoes together and...

WHAM!

The blast I'd experienced back in the Not-Really-a-Wizard's palace was nothing compared to this. We whirled and zoomed, in darkness and flashes of blinding light. Then, suddenly, we hit the ground with a thud, and I could smell chicken feed.

"Toto!" someone yelled accusingly.

I opened my eyes. We were in the farmyard, and Auntem was stomping toward me with a grim expression on her face. Happy dashed around to hide behind the other side of the barn.

We made it! I wanted to dance. *We're home!* I didn't care whether Auntem was mad at me. It would never matter ever again. We were home. I'd brought my girl home.

Auntem yanked the shoe out of my mouth and wagged her finger at me.

"How could you run off and something something? Dorothy went to look for you and never came back!" Her voice was so piercing I thought my eardrums would explode.

What was wrong with her? She should have been all excited to see her girl again.

Then I realized I couldn't smell Dorothy at all.

Chapter 32

I looked around and saw no sign of her. There was a new house standing where the old one had been, and I ran up to see if she was inside. The door was shut, and the screen didn't have a hole in it that I could push open like the old one had.

I turned around. Auntem was crying—sobbing, really—and Unclehenry came out of the barn and gathered her in a long hug. I tried to figure out what had happened. Had Dorothy been blasted somewhere else?

Or had she been left behind because she wasn't touching the shoes?

"A-caw!" Eggy crowed as she strutted across the farmyard. "There he sits, as pretty as you please. The little rat-dog that killed Dorothy."

"What?" I shook my head. "I didn't kill Dorothy." At least I didn't think I had. What if banging the shoes together had blasted me into Kansas and Dorothy into a million pieces? I tried not to think about it. She must still be back in Oz.

A wise old draft horse leaned his head over the fence and fixed me in a cold gaze.

217

"If the girl hadn't gone to look for you, she would have sheltered in the stormcellar with her aunt and uncle. Instead, she was caught in the storm. You're an evil little beast and not welcome here any longer. So, take your wild friend and go."

"You heard him," Eggy squawked "Go!"

Before I realized what was happening, all the chickens and roosters had circled me and started pushing me out of the yard toward the road.

"Happy!" I barked. "Get the—"

I was trying to tell him to get the shoe Auntem had taken from me. If we banged the shoes together again, we could return to Oz, get Dorothy and bring her back.

But as soon as Happy came around the corner of the barn and saw all those chickens, he didn't wait to hear what I had to say. With a predatory howl of glee, he dropped the shoe he was carrying and took off after three fat hens who'd lagged behind the rest.

"No!" I barked frantically. "Don't chase the chickens!"

Of course, he didn't hear me. I couldn't even hear myself. The squawking was bad enough, but all the other animals started lowing and bellowing loud enough to wake the dead.

"Oinkaah!" the pig snorted. "Wolf in the yard."

"Mooove back! Watch out for the wolf," the cow nearest to the fence warned the others.

"Toto, you have taken up with the wrong crowd," the horse concluded, sadly shaking his head.

Happy dashed by at full speed, obviously having the time of his life with chickens dodging this way and that to get away from him.

"Stop!" I yelled uselessly as he raced around the farmyard chanting "Chicken, chicken, chicken!"

I'd been there myself. I knew the joy, the excitement, the euphoria that comes from chasing those brainless bags of feathers. I knew he wouldn't listen.

But he had to.

Because Unclehenry had come out of the barn carrying his shotgun.

"Happy!"

He didn't even slow down.

I swallowed hard to stop the panic rising in my throat. Think! Okay, we needed to get the shoes together and get back to Oz. I could work on that, right?

I went over to retrieve the shoe Happy had dropped by the barn, trying to ignore the "click, click" as Unclehenry loaded shells into his gun. Once I had Happy's shoe, I had to find the one Auntem had taken away from me. I couldn't see it anywhere on the ground, but it could have been trampled under swirling masses of hysterical chickens. How could I find it in this mess?

Unclehenry set the box of shotgun shells on the lantern shelf, and I turned away so I wouldn't see him take aim.

Of course! Humans always set things down on shelves, or something like a shelf. There were no shelves out in the farmyard, but there were steps leading up to the henhouse. Those were like shelves. I ran over to look, and there was the shoe, sitting right on the top step. Now all I had to do was get through the mass of crazed chickens to reach it.

"Toto!" Unclehenry bellowed as I jumped into the fray. Well, as least if he was angry at me for getting in the way that meant he didn't hate me enough to want to shoot me. Or maybe he did, but he just wanted a clear shot at Happy first. Either way, I was distracting him, and that was good.

Of course, I realized as I picked up the second shoe in the corner of my mouth, the one I needed to distract was Happy. But he couldn't hear me over all the noise, and he wouldn't slow down to look at me. There was only one thing I could think of that would get him to pay attention to me, and that would be if I turned myself into a large succulent pork chop.

The magic shoes might have been able to do it, but I really didn't want to end up as dinner for a wolf who had trouble multi-tasking.

Would a bone do it? I had one buried in the soft ground by the water trough. I'd been saving it for an emergency, and this was more emergency than I had ever dreamed of.

Carrying both shoes carefully, I staggered over to the water trough, set them down, dug up the bone and held it up in my mouth. My saliva should help bring out the smell.

"Chicken, chicken, chicken," Happy chanted.

No! My mind screamed. *Think pork chop. Smell the pork chop.* Be *the pork chop.*

"Chicken, chicken, chicken!" Happy insisted as he raced by.

I dropped the bone so I could yell "Pork chop!" in my loudest bark.

"Chicken, chicken, PORK CHOP!" Happy wheeled around suddenly, lunged toward me and snatched the bone.

"Very good," I said. "Now put it down and pick up the smelly shoe."

Happy shook his head.

"There are better pork chop bones in Oz," I insisted.

He looked unconvinced.

"And no one knows if there are pork chops in heaven," I pointed out. "Which is where you will be after Unclehenry hits you with a shotgun blast."

The bone fell out of his mouth as he turned and saw the barrels of Unclehenry's gun aimed straight at his head. With lightning speed, he picked up the shoe in front of him and charged into me. I barely got my mouth on the edge of my shoe as the one Happy was carrying smacked into it.

With the same whirl of light and dark, we were back in Oz.

And Dorothy was still yelling at me.

Chapter 33

It was as if we'd never left. She showed no surprise at all that we had disappeared and then reappeared, just a lot of anger. Her voice sounded harsh and nasty. She sounded older, too. Almost like a grown-up person who had forgotten how to have fun.

I dropped the shiny witch shoe in front of her and nodded for Happy to do the same. Then I nudged the shoes closer to Dorothy, hoping she'd take the hint and put them on. We could bang those shoes all we wanted, but if Dorothy wasn't wearing them, she'd be left behind again.

Instead of looking at them, Dorothy turned away and looked toward the sky. Out toward the horizon, I could see a small ice cream cone with a flat bottom. Dorothy wanted to be in that ice cream cone.

"Put on the shoes," I barked. If only she could understand me! I bent down, put my nose against the shoes and shoved them gently but firmly against her toes.

At first, this got no reaction, but after I barked again, Dorothy turned back to look at me. Tears sparkled in the corners of her eyes, and I could smell the rage and distress streaming out with each breath she took. The sadness would have broken my heart if I hadn't been certain everything would be alright once she put on the shoes.

I barked again and wagged my tail, concentrating as hard as I could.

Pick up the shoes!

And she did! As if she had read my mind, Dorothy reached down and grabbed the shiny witch shoes.

Then she flung them into the water.

"No!" I howled. "No! We need those shoes."

I jumped onto the top of the stone wall surrounding the giant bath. For a moment, the shoes floated on the surface of the water like two witchy boats, but soon one of them began to tip; and I knew that, any second, it would sink to the bottom. Then we'd have no chance of getting home.

"Happy," I barked over my shoulder, "can you reach them?"

"I dunno." He jumped up next to me and stretched his neck out as far as he could, but the shoes floated well out of his reach.

"Can wolves swim?" The water was dark, and it was impossible to tell how deep it was.

He shook his head. "No. Can terriers swim?"

"I don't know." I'd never been in water over my head, and there weren't a lot of terriers in the farmyard—or Oz—for me to discuss swimming with.

"Uh-oh," he muttered.

My heart leapt into my throat as one of the shoes began to fill with water. Already it was starting to slip under the surface.

Dorothy had her back to us. Since she'd thrown the shoes in, she wasn't likely to take them back out again no matter how much I barked. She also wouldn't be able to pull me out if I jumped in and found out I couldn't swim. I might drown in the cold, wet awfulness of the giant bath.

But if I didn't save those shoes, Dorothy would never get back to Kansas. She had given up her chance to go home in the balloon just to look for me. I had to do what I could for her.

Bracing myself for the chill, I crouched then leaped toward the sinking shoe.

The water was so cold I didn't even notice how wet it was. I didn't care if my hair was soppy and matted. I couldn't breathe. My head was above water, but all the air had been sucked out of me.

Just when I thought I would freeze into an ice cube and sink straight to the bottom, I saw the shoe. It was only a few feet away, with the heel submerged and the toe bobbing gently on the surface.

Run! Something in me urged. *Get that shoe!*

I couldn't really run in the water, but the running motion of my legs propelled me forward.

"Hey, man!" Happy called gleefully from the wall. "I guess terriers *can* swim."

Swim? Was that what I was doing? Well, at least I wasn't getting washed.

As soon as I got near the sinking shoe, I grabbed it in my teeth, turned and paddled back to the wall. Happy reached down and took it from me.

"One more to go," I gasped as I headed back out into the great expanse of water. I tried not to think about how deep it might be, or to imagine what creatures might be lurking in the dark water. I just kept running. I mean, swimming.

The second shoe was easier to carry because it wasn't as full of water, but I was pretty tired by the time I got back to the wall. I was so tired, in fact, I didn't even object when Happy reached down and plucked me out of the water by the nape of my neck as if I were a puppy.

A wet strand of fur flopped into my eyes, and I couldn't see for a moment. When I shook it out, I saw that Dorothy and all the short people were looking down at the ground.

"Who're they bowing to?" Happy wondered aloud.

"Bowing?" I asked. "What's that?"

"People look down when an alpha-someone-important arrives," Happy explained. "It's, like, how they show respect. The Witch used to make people bow down to her."

"So, does that mean that lady is a witch?" I nodded toward a woman coming toward us wearing a big puffy dress that looked like a lampshade. She was the only one not bowing down. "That's the lady who made us start walking on the brick road."

"Hey, man." Happy put his nose up in the air and gave a big sniff. "I think that's a Good Witch."

"I've never heard of a Good Witch."

He nodded toward her. "Just smell, man."

I pointed my nose in her direction and gave a tentative sniff. The scent of spiced apple pie came distinctly to my nostrils. It reminded me of how everything smelled when we first arrived. When we had first seen the lampshade lady.

She sure *smelled* like a Good Witch.

I shook the water out of my hair and jumped off the wall so I could run over and get a closer sniff. But as I was running toward her, she walked right past me to the wall. Her dress sleeves sparkled in the sunlight as she reached to pick up the witch shoes. Was she going to take them for herself? Oh, I had been a fool to trust the smell of apple pie!

But, no, my nose was right after all. The lampshade lady was, indeed, a good witch. She handed the magic shoes to Dorothy.

"Do not cry, my girl," she said in a gentle voice. "These shoes will take you home."

Immediately, Dorothy stepped out of her new slippers and put on the old witch's shoes, even though they were dripping wet. I sighed. So, the good witch was going to get all the credit for thinking of the magic shoes, even though I'd been trying to get Dorothy to put them back on all day.

Oh, well, at least we were finally going home.

After Dorothy put the shoes on, she started hugging Strawman and Metal Man and Big Cat.

"Oh," she said, kind of laughing and crying at the same time, "if I'd known, I could have gone home anytime."

"But then I wouldn't have realized how smart I was, even without brains," Strawman said.

"And I wouldn't have realized that I can still care for others even without a heart," Metal Man added joyously.

"And I wouldn't have realized that I..." Big Cat stopped and whirled around. "Something grabbed my tail. I know I felt something grab my tail."

Well, he had courage when he most needed it, and I guess that was enough.

"So, you see, Dorothy," Strawman concluded, "your time in Oz helped us a lot. Thank you."

What about *my* time in Oz? I wanted to ask, but as Dorothy picked me up, I realized it was okay if they never acknowledged my help. Dorothy and I were a team. When they thanked Dorothy, they were thanking me, too.

Dorothy smiled, though there were tears in the corners of her eyes.

"I'm ready to go home now, but I'll miss you all."

I was surprised to realize I might miss them a bit, too.

And I knew I would miss Happy.

"Hey," I barked as he came up next to Dorothy. "Thanks for everything."

He wagged his tale like a puppy. "You're welcome, man."

I wagged, too. "I'd tell you to come visit us in Kansas sometime, but..."

I think we both had the same image in our minds of Unclehenry and his shotgun.

Happy laughed. "No, thanks. I think I'll stay right here. The chickens were fun, though."

"Yeah." I nodded in agreement. "And it's time for me to get back to them. You take care of things around here, okay?"

"I'll do my best," Happy promised as he eyed a basket of smoked fish someone had set down on the stone wall.

Dorothy leaned over and smooshed her lips into my hair, which I don't really like, but I put up with it because I can tell she only does it when she's very happy with me. Maybe she did realize I had something to do with the shoes after all.

"What do I do with the shoes to get home?" she asked the Good Witch.

"Just think of where you want to go..." the lampshade lady began.

"And bang your heels together," I barked. The lampshade lady said the same thing, and Dorothy really listened to her, but I pretended that, just this once, she had listened to me.

With a little wave to everyone, she smacked her heels together. There was that blast of light and darkness.

And then I could smell chickens.

Epilogue

I don't think I need to tell anyone how happy we were to be back home, and how happy Auntem and Unclehenry were to see Dorothy. They even petted me, which they don't do often. And although Unclehenry kept his shotgun nearby for a couple of days, eventually he stopped looking for stray wolves in the farmyard.

I discovered that the yard smelled even better than I remembered. And I started burying all my bones there, and vowed never again to dig up the neighbor's flowers. Besides, that neighbor kind of looked like the Witch, and she did have a wickedly sharp pitchfork. Witches might melt back in Oz, but if the neighbor went after me with that pitchfork again, all the water in the Kansas probably wouldn't slow her down.

We settled back into our daily routine of playing and working and napping. Dorothy was as messy as ever, throwing sticks all over the place so I had to keep cleaning them up. The chickens never again called me a "rodent," because I think they were afraid I'd bring Happy back if they made me mad.

One day, as I yawned and settled down for my afternoon nap on the porch, I thought gratefully about the help we'd received from the three wise guys and the wolves and all the other creatures we'd met in Oz. Without their help, we probably never would have made it back.

I had really learned to appreciate this treeless windswept Kansas prairie we called home. There truly was no place like home for burying bones and chasing chickens and snuggling with your pet girl. No place like home. No place like home. No place like...no place... no...zzzzzzzzzzzzzzzzzzzzzzzzzzz.

End

ABOUT THE AUTHORS

K.D. HAYS and MEG WEIDMAN are a mother-daughter team who aspire to be professional rollercoaster riders and who can tell you exactly what not to put in your pockets when you ride El Toro at Six Flags.

Meg is studying art in a middle school magnet program. For fun, she jumps on a precision jump rope team and reads anything not associated with school work. K.D. Hays, who writes historical fiction under the name Kate Dolan, has been writing professionally since 1992. She holds a law degree from the University of Richmond and consequently hopes that her children will pursue studies in more prestigious fields such as plumbing or waste management.

They live in a suburb of Baltimore where the weather is ideally suited for the four major seasons—riding roller-coasters in the spring and fall, waterslides in the summer and snow tubes in the winter.

Although Meg resents the fact her mother has dragged her to every historical site within a 200-mile radius, she will consent to dress in colonial garb and participate in living history demonstrations if she is allowed to be a laundry thief.

ABOUT THE ARTIST

APRIL MARTINEZ was born in the Philippines and raised in San Diego, California, daughter to a US Navy chef and a US postal worker, sibling to one younger sister. From as far back as she can remember, she has always doodled and loved art, but her parents never encouraged her to consider it as a career path, suggesting instead that she work for the county. So, she attended the University of California in San Diego, earned a cum laude bachelor's degree in literature/writing and entered the workplace as a regular office worker.

For years, she went from job to job, dissatisfied that she couldn't make use of her creative tendencies, until she started working as an imaging specialist for a big book and magazine publishing house in Irvine and began learning the trade of graphic design. From that point on, she worked as a graphic designer and webmaster at subsequent day jobs while doing freelance art and illustration at night.

In 2003, April discovered the e-publishing industry. She responded to an ad looking for e-book cover artists and was soon in the business of cover art and art direction. Since then, she has created hundreds of book covers, both electronic and print, for several publishing houses, earning awards and recognition in the process. Two years into it, she was able to give up the day job and work from home.

April Martinez now lives with her cat in Orange County, California, as a full-time freelance artist/illustrator and graphic designer.

Made in the USA
Charleston, SC
17 September 2010